"Mad genius at work."
Book Reviews by Elizabeth A. White

"Bergen has the perfect pitch for witty dialog and cultural references, and his characters are fascinating people you'll want to hang out with... but he also creates some of the most wildly imaginative places ever encountered in fiction."
Chris Rhatigan, editor of *All Due Respect* and *Pulp Ink*

"A great read, really fun and different."
NerdSpan

"Bergen's characters embody very relatable human frustrations and impulses... these arch, nostalgic vignettes also showcase identifiable human flaws and imperfections, investing them with more dimension than their humourous pulp trappings outwardly suggest."
Australian Comics Journal

"A *lot* to love here."
All-Comic

"Nobody else today writes with the same dark wit, style or mad creativity."
Christopher Black, *Available in Any Colour*

Small Change

A Casebook of Scherer and Miller,
Investigators of the Paranormal
and Supermundane

Small Change

A Casebook of Scherer and Miller,
Investigators of the Paranormal
and Supermundane

Andrez Bergen

Winchester, UK
Washington, USA

First published by Roundfire Books, 2015
Roundfire Books is an imprint of John Hunt Publishing Ltd., Laurel House, Station Approach,
Alresford, Hants, SO24 9JH, UK
office1@jhpbooks.net
www.johnhuntpublishing.com
www.roundfire-books.com

For distributor details and how to order please visit the 'Ordering' section on our website.

Text copyright: Andrez Bergen 2014

ISBN: 978 1 78535 219 5
Library of Congress Control Number: 2015946053

A CIP catalogue record for this book is available from the British Library.

Design: Stuart Davies

Printed in the USA by Edwards Brothers Malloy

We operate a distinctive and ethical publishing philosophy in all
areas of our business, from our global network of authors to
production and worldwide distribution.

CONTENTS

for Rock Hudson and Susan Saint James

1: A BIT OVER TWO YEARS AGO

"A zombie. I hate zombies."

I leaned back against the barn wall. Job was going to be the death of me. The job, or my partner, Suzie — and I use the term in its loosest sense.

"Actually, I don't think he qualifies as a zombie, per se."

There she was, on tiptoes, right in my ear. Why on earth she had to tag along, I never understood. I operated better alone — her old man knew that. Why couldn't this blonde busybody get the message?

I glanced down. "What?"

"More a relative of Lazarus, you know? The guy that was reanimated by Jesus Christ."

"No, I don't know. Are you going to give me another diatribe in the middle of a scene?"

"Well, I think it's important in our business to be accurate. If we went around claiming succubae were incubae, or silver bullets stopped vampires, well, we wouldn't be in business all that long, y'know?"

"*My* business."

"Who pays the bills, Roy?"

I could feel the acid steep in my gut, brewing down there in oak barrels aplenty. "Not now, okay? Timing." Pushed both index fingers in my ears.

It was right then that our new playmate Lazarus rounded the corner, so I unplugged, settled my Smith & Wesson Model 10 in the crook of the guy's neck, and fired off a single shot. Didn't want to waste bullets — no need to be further still in Suzie's clutching debt. The man reeled backwards and lay on the ground, inert.

"Too easy. Lazarus didn't rise twice, did he?"

"Don't think so. Then again, I've never actually read the book, just heard about it."

"You're feeding me second-hand yarns? So much for accuracy." I stepped slowly over to the body. Even in the crap half-light, just before dawn, I could see it was twitching. "Crap. He's not dead."

"Oh, Christ!"

"Will you stop bringing him into it?"

"All right, all right. What should we do? Do you think we should drive a stake through his heart just in case?"

"He's not Bela Lugosi."

The man groaned there on the ground. Slowly sat up, clutching his throat, and placed a wobbly head between his knees. I considered popping off another round, but decided otherwise. Stood awkwardly with Suzie, waiting.

"You all right, mister?" Suzie finally asked.

"Look what you did to my neck," the man cried out between splayed legs. I was impressed he could still enunciate. Definitely wasn't a zombie. "You...you bungled it! You and your stupid attempt to kill me!"

Suzie shifted from one runner to another. "Not me," my rock-solid partner assured him.

"Coward," I muttered.

She frowned over the rim of her bookish glasses, but the expression had little room to stand on such a damnably young face. "Haven't you caused enough trouble?"

"That's right, blame me." I blew out loudly. "Look, sorry, but we're here because we got a job to do, a client to make happy."

"Who—?"

"Well, now, that wouldn't be very professional, handing out names like speeding tickets. Anyway, this nameless client reported a fiend mutilating his flock. Local police reckoned it was a feral dog or cat, but our client suspected otherwise — and then he spotted someone on two legs. Given it's the middle of the night and you just stuffed your face with some defenseless lamb, we'd be excused for thinking you were the culprit."

The speech was a longer one than I usually made. It exhausted me.

At that, Lazarus cried.

Yes, he bawled. Suzie and I looked at one another. Aside from blubbering there was an ungainly silence. The girl handed him a tissue, but I broke the peace first.

"Well, this is comical. What now?"

"Apologize?" my partner said.

"Apologize?"

"You could try. I'm not sure I can stand much more of this."

"The devil, you say? I'm not going to apologize — don't you remember why we're here and what this guy just did? What do we tell our client? 'We found your bogeyman, and we shot the bastard, but then he sobbed a lot, we had a change of mind, and kissed and made up'?"

"Well, that's a no-brainer. Who's going to hire people who sympathize with their cases?"

Lazarus held up his hand. "Will you two be quiet? You're giving me a splitting headache — I'm already in enough pain."

"Sorry, I haven't domesticated her yet."

"Fat chance." The girl crossed her arms and looked away.

"Who are you people?"

On cue, like she'd been desperately awaiting an invite, Suzie's body unravelled and she handed him the baby-blue business card. "Scherer and Miller, Investigators of the Paranormal and Supermundane."

Lazarus looked up. Tough to mark his age — late fifties? — before he died. A bloated face that looked to me a lot like dead actor Peter Lorre, but mark that down to late nights with a bottle of rye and American International flicks for company.

"Who's Scherer?" he inquired, in goddamned polite fashion.

"That would be me," I said.

"So you're Miller?"

"Er...no. That would be — *was*— my dad. I'm Suzie."

Lazarus leaned over and vomited up a pool of gunk, most of it blood, but I also spotted bits and pieces of sheep.

"You do know raw lamb is prone to parasites?" Suzie admonished him. "Ought to be more careful."

"I'm sorry. I can't help myself," Lazarus bawled. He was blubbering again, a grown ghoul shedding tears. This was ridiculous.

"Well, next time. Just for the record, are you craving brains?"

Suzie pushed frames back up her maddeningly cute button nose, and then conjured up a pad and pencil. "I want to be sure we're dealing here with Lazarus syndrome, or if it's localized zombiefication."

"What the devil does it matter? Ever since I woke up in that awful morgue, somehow alive again, I've been ravenous, craving meat, hungry, desperate, mad—"

Another point-blank thirty-eight special, this time in his left eye, killed that appetite. "My, my, my! Such a lot of guts around town and so few brains."

"Ew," Suzie said.

"Think we can mark down this case as closed."

"Dad would've been more prudent."

"Your old man's dead."

"Even so, wasn't that a bit gung-ho? Maybe we could've helped out the poor man, y'know?"

"We're not in the business of helping these spooks. Count your blessings — at least we didn't have to waste any silverware. C'mon. I'm dying for something to eat."

"*Ew.*"

Who was it that conjured up the dumb expression about there being no rest for the wicked?

I didn't dare ask this of Suzie, since she'd likely put her head down into books or surf online until she had the answer down pat – thence to bore me with the details about Shakespeare or Isaiah or whoever it damn well was.

As a P.I. her dad hadn't the necessary skill to stay above water, but as a concept-man he'd hit pay-dirt, even if the money rolled in posthumously. Who else cottoned on that there were so many ghouls in the world?

So, anyway, it should come as no surprise that, since business was booming, we had another engagement two nights later. Least on this occasion it wasn't a rural gig. No, we had a mansion before us.

We rolled up by taxi since neither Suzie nor I had a license or a boiler to go with said paperwork.

The expansive garden up front was an overgrown affair that hadn't seen a hoe since, I don't know, the turn of the millennium? And the rundown, double-story Edwardian villa would've been quite at ease filling in for Miss Havisham's stomping ground.

We entered via the front door after I picked two locks, but that process was delayed as Suzie insisted upon buzzing the doorbell, and then knocking several times. Once she was sure no manservant or ring-in Renfield was going to answer, I whipped out a hairpin — "Ouch!" she griped, trying to hold her 'do in place — and borrowed her Diner's Club card.

The next hour we spent exploring this Château Videz from top to bottom. All we found were lifeless rooms with discoloured sheeting covering the furniture. The place looked like it hadn't been lived in since that yard got its last manicure. The only unusual addition was this dated ghetto-blaster with a compact-disc collection that included LPs by Michael Jackson and Steely Dan.

So, from the bottom we travelled further still, into a place

Suzie wasn't so keen to enter: The cellar. Expecting to find racks of dusty old bottles, we instead came across a dusty coffin made of oak propped on this cement slab in the middle of the large space. The only decoration was an overhead crystal chandelier.

"Why d'you suppose they have a chandelier in the basement?" Suzie said.

"Must've doubled-up as a ballroom."

"Seriously?"

"How the devil should I know?"

Ignoring her, I approached the wooden casket.

"Holy water ready!" Suzie shouted in that quiet space.

"Shhh." Having raised the lid, I found our man dozing on a velveteen cushion. "Stake," I whispered in my best surgeon's tone. My assistant handed me 'Mr. Pointy'.

Now for the messy part — the part where I usually end up with splinters or a blister from gripping the bugger too hard.

I placed the stake on the chest just so, where the heart's supposed to be. In the early days I used to bring an anatomy diagram to make sure I got it right. You really don't want to get it wrong. These spooks wake up grumpy, and they're likely to take out their crankiness on the nearest bystander — that's right, you with the silly wooden tent peg in your hand.

Having positioned the thing, I lifted up the mallet, prepared to strike, and—

"Wait! Wait a moment!"

—Missed the stake completely. Heard a couple of ribs break instead. Shit.

Suzie stuck her head into my field of vision, between me and the corpse with the busted-up bones. "Are you one hundred percent positive this guy is a vampire?" she asked in that cloying, up-and-down tone of hers that drove me to distraction. It was like conversing with a verbal yoyo.

"Suzie, move. Now. No time for safety checks."

"Well, I don't know, I think we ought to create the time,

y'know, just to be sure? Lawsuits and all. We don't want to do this, and then find out after that we nailed the wrong man. Cadaver. Vampire...*er* — you know what I mean."

"I do. And I think we can skip the litmus test, thanks to you."

"Really?" The giddy girl actually looked happy. "Why?"

A pair of hands rounded her neck from behind, and started to squeeze — hard. Something I'd dreamed about doing over the past six months. Suzie's glasses fell to the floor as she went in the other direction, up in the air. She was gasping, wheezing, and still trying to talk. God, shut up.

For dramatic effect, fangs lifted her further — which was when Suzie gripped the chandelier.

That's the problem with vampires.

They live so long they get grand notions about themselves, move from holes in the ground into crypts with marble slabs, and on into houses, and then — if they live a few centuries like this boy — migrate up to mansions with crystal chandeliers stuck to the ceiling. In cellars, no less.

The same very thing Suzie was hanging onto now for dear life, frustrating the vampire, since he was still holding her aloft and couldn't exactly lob the girl across the room when she had a half-decent grip on something.

Meanwhile, he looked straight down at me with my stick, a wide-open space between us inviting another go at his heart.

Not such a bright boy, this one. Should've just let the kid go. Instead, he stood there with hands in the air, mouth wide open with surprise. I should've guessed this'd be an easy round — the vampire dressed in duds from the '80s, he still owned CDs, and I could imagine him indulging in moonwalks across dance floors in front of horrified clubbing clientele.

"Roy!" I heard Suzie shout.

Damn — thought the vampire was still arresting vocal cords. "You can hold her tighter," I hissed at the ghoul in a low voice. "Help me out here."

"What?" The vampire looked more confused. Definitely well past any use-by date.

"Roy, when you're ready."

"I don't know, Suze," I said, holding vamp's eyes with mine. "Are we one hundred percent sure bozo qualifies?"

"Actually, I'd say one or two percent above that. But only just."

"What is wrong with you people?" Dracula fumed, and I could see he'd made the prolonged decision to let the girl go. Playtime was over.

I plunged the stake into his stomach first. "That was for fun," I said, as the spook shrieked with pain. I pulled the tool out and stuck it right where the heart was supposed to be, behind a couple of fractured ribs. "And that's for offensive fashion."

There was no exploding, no accelerated decrepitude, not even a decent yodel. The vampire fell backwards into his coffin, holding the stake, and lay there stiff. Cue lacklustre applause. Fall of shabby curtain. Blah, blah.

Suzie was still hanging from the chandelier above me, runners a few inches from my nose.

"Did we win?" she asked.

"Yeah, yeah. Don't we always?"

"You'll catch me?"

I thought hard about that one.

Don't know about you, but I'm not a golfing aficionado. I played once when I was eighteen — Artie suckered me into a game with one of his clients — and it involved a day's rambling in 44-degree heat that left me hospitalized. Sunstroke, the quacks said.

"It's alien," Art's daughter Suzie said now, a decade later. The man'd suckered me with her as well.

This latest grating comment caused me to glance her way across the green. "Alien?"

"Alien."

"You certain?"

"Course I'm not certain. No one would be."

"Then why say it?"

"Because 'alien' is quicker and easier than saying 'of unknown, likely extraterrestrial origin, though at this stage I have no evidence to prove same'."

"You think?"

"I *know*. I'm out of breath." Having crouched down in moist bunker sand, Suzie rotated this small foreign device we'd found, the same dimensions as a Colt 1911 pistol, between her hands. Similar size it may've been, but definitely this didn't look like a .45. "Furthermore, going by the odd technology, I'd say this's been constructed by some new race we've never before encountered."

"As opposed," I muttered, superior in my place standing above her on the green, "to one made by those we have."

"Exactly."

"Right."

Inspecting the gadget the girl might've been, but she also started humming something — I couldn't be sure, but it sounded like the Commodores' 1970s standard 'Three Times a Lady'. And then the words hammered this home — in Suzie's skewed adaptation.

In this early-morning darkness it was easy to scowl without being spotted, a freedom of facial movement I usually avoided.

"Anyone tell you, Suze, that you have the dulcet singing tone of two alley cats in a death-fight for dominance?"

"You're just jealous."

"No. I'm not." I jumped down to squat beside her. "So, what's this got to do with the remains of our client?"

'Remains' being overly optimistic language — dead guy was a scattering of ashes, in the shape of a man, over on clean-cut grass.

"Well, Roy, this looks like some kind of weapon. A disintegrator ray, p'raps."

"Obviously."

"Oh, you already figured that out?"

"Sweetheart, we could squeeze what's left of our man into an ashtray."

"I guess. Huh."

Suzie removed glasses, pushing back a tuft of hair, and casually pointed E.T.'s thingamajig at yours truly. At least I assumed it was pointed my way — this was a jumble of wires and tubes that better resembled a golden-era homemade ham radio that'd been jumped by a toaster and cut down to clunky pocket-size. She could've had the thing backwards.

"Easy there," I warned. "Prefer to hang onto my head. And I still need yours."

This caused the girl to lower what we assumed to be a weapon, this dopey smile on her mush. "Really? Is that true, Roy?"

"Sadly? Yep."

Any further pointless admissions were cut off by an incandescent glow that filled the eastern sky, and this wasn't the sun making an early arrival. The source appeared to be a tiny white dot that soared heavenward, trailing sparks.

Without thinking, I'd removed my hat. "And, I'd say, there goes the perp."

"Our chance to meet and greet a new race," sighed Suzie,

"gone in a flash."

"Along with the paycheque, and a previously unblemished case record."

"Still."

"I don't care if they're from this planet or another dimension — émigrés're all the same. You can't trust the bastards." I glanced sidelong at my partner and removed the contraption still pressed between her fingers. "Then again, I s'pose we can hock this thing on eBay."

Suzie looked horrified. "As a weapon?"

"As art, baby, as art. Get a better price."

Sometimes we worked cases back-to-back. On other occasions I had a couple of weeks to recuperate and repair wits damaged in the course of duty.

This one came three weeks after the golfing escapade, yet I still hadn't adequately steeled myself.

"Roy, what's your verdict?"

That was the classic Suzie whine — quizzing before I'd had time to soak in sights, let alone this diorama of death on a floor before us the moment we entered the basement laboratory through one busted-up door.

Busted because it'd been in the way — locked from the inside and the landlady didn't have a key. In splintered pieces thanks to my shoulder, which now ached like all hell. Blame Suzie. This time round she had neither hairpin nor credit card.

"Dunno. Place reeks?" I said, sarcasm lining the retort as if a ham-fisted seamstress in some Hong Kong back alley had tailored it up. Yet Suzie still missed that.

"No, aside from the pungent chemicals I mean."

With her left hot-pink Converse All Star shoe the girl cautiously prodded an elderly horizontal corpse lying on dull linoleum in the middle of this room, a broken beaker beside outstretched left hand. The lab-rat had a pained look permanently etched upon his face and I knew that expression well. I'm sure we shared matching crisscrossing lines even if this geezer had a half-century lead.

"Professor Jones here," Suzie went on in that up/down tone that sent a shiver carousing my spine. "How d'you think he died?"

"Gimme a moment."

"What, are you slowing down in your old age?"

"No, but I am getting flashbacks from *Raiders of the Lost Ark*."

"How so?"

I rubbed my chin, ignoring her. "Could be a classic case of hen-peck."

Crouching beside our man, I placed my brown Stetson atop a brown-trousered right knee to inspect this body for clues. Light was crap — all I had to work off was one flickering Bunsen burner and a Tesla coil electrical transformer straight out of those Frankenstein flicks Universal did in the 1930s, along with a UV-C germicidal lamp above an enclosed laminar flow cabinet.

"Chooks?" my partner squawked. "You think?"

When I glanced over I saw her scouring every nook and cranny, all panic. I stopped watching to rub tired eyes. "It's the expression, Suze. Hen-pecked husband — you know? Not literal. Chill. We're hardly going to discover homicidal hens."

"Oh, well, that's a relief." Susie had out her accursed notepad and jotted something down. "No chickens," she mumbled. "What, then?"

Time to bounce a question back. "Was the Prof married?"

Suzie scanned notes. "A widower. Three times over."

"How long till the old battle-axe upstairs calls in the cops?"

"You're talking about Dad's sister — my aunt."

"Same question."

Peering at the ceiling, my partner shrugged as she pushed blonde hair behind the left ear. A habit I'd picked up on. "Said she'd give us fifteen minutes."

Huh. Quarter of an hour too long in this confined space. "What's dead guy to her? Tennant only, or geriatric toy boy?"

"*Ew*. Is that important?"

"No. But helps me to think seeing you squirm."

Having adjusted the frames on her nose, my girl stared back. "You're a sad individual, Roy. I feel for you."

The devil she did — kid was getting frisky, up on hind legs and cracking foxy. I don't know why, but this put me out.

"One more thing," I said. "Why is it we're here?"

"Daisy knows what we do."

"What *do* we do?"

"You know."

"All that nonsense, re: investigating the paranormal?"

"Not to forget the supermundane. Yep."

I sighed and stood. "Are we talking family-rates on this job?"

"Mmm." Suzie suddenly sounded vague. "She's just as curious regarding the mystery of what happened."

"Not often a corpse locks the door from the inside."

"Exactly."

"Unless the old coot did himself in. Which means the police'd be far more appropriate than us. They are anyway — we're hacks."

"Speak for yourself."

"Think I may've been doing just that. I might be a hack, but you're the Plus One."

Judging by her next comment, Suzie had taken to ignoring my barbs.

"D'you think it was suicide, Roy?"

"Either that, or clever foul play."

That got Suzie agitated again. "Those chickens?"

Bingo. I smiled to myself. "Foul, not fowl. Anyway, I'm steering suicide's way like you figure. With all the chemicals in here, something like that'd be a piece of cake — and I'd like to know what was in this broken beaker."

I placed the hat back on my head and walked over to examine instead a work bench: scouring test-tube clamps, a Florence flask and twin Erlenmeyers containing some ugly-coloured fluid, evaporating dishes and tubes of assorted size. A row of big glass jars on shelves circumnavigated the lab. Things in formaldehyde like cat fœti, pickled mandrake root, floating toads, a five-fingered monkey's — "What do we call that? Do monkeys have hands or paws?"

"Hands. I think. Is that important?"

"Nah, just curious."

There was a set of objects on a shelf at head-height for Suzie, the level of my shoulder, with a white drop-sheet obscuring them. I crossed the room and drew the rag aside.

"Nuts," I said.

"Nuts?"

"Check this out. Human heads. Three of 'em."

I was ogling three lookers on ice — without the frost. The one on the left minus hair, her partner in the middle a brunette, and our right-hand decoration boasting a red 'do cut short. Yes, a trio of ravishing beauties — the fact they didn't have a chassis between them was a drawback, but you take what you're gifted. They even had coloured Christmas-bulb electrodes woven about their heads.

Suzie minced up to lean close. "Oh, wow. Women. Decapitated clean as a whistle, surgically by the looks. Pretty lights. And are these miniature 30-Watt speakers attached to each pedestal? Why?"

"Who cares? ... So the Prof was some kind of Blackbeard, collecting scalps with the heads attached."

"Bluebeard. Blackbeard was a pirate."

"Collector of fine goods all the same." I glanced my partner's way. "How many wives did you say he had?"

"Three."

"Liked to dip his hand in different pies too. There I was thinking the old geezer was boring."

"Is this legal?"

I frowned at Suzie. "I'd say not."

"Depends whose head it is."

That was the moment one of the skulls, Kojak, opened its eyes and lobbed interference to our mundane dialogue via a tinny tone coming out of a 30-Watt speaker. "It's mine."

Neither Suzie nor I had much to say for several seconds thereafter. I'll give cred to my partner, however — she broke the silence first.

"Who're you?"

"Why, I'm Mrs. Jones of course."

"The first one. The veteran head." This came from another noggin, the brunette. Seniority carbuncle here sounded less respectful, more uttered with venom. "Hence the lack of hair."

"Oh, shut up," the first head complained.

"Who're you?" Suzie asked the second, apparently stuck on repeat.

"Mrs. Jones."

"But I thought she—"

Our brunette scowled. "First wife, second wife. Get with it."

"Temper, temper," Baldie said.

"Shut your fat gob."

"They're always like this." A new voice had entered the fray, this one an equally thin, metallic sound coming from the redhead to the right.

Before Suzie could use her standard a third time, I butted in. "You would be Mrs. Jones III."

"That's right, sugar. The new, improved model."

Brunette rolled eyes. "And about as smart as a third leg."

"Glad we agree on something," Baldie said.

Brunette: "That what you think?"

Baldie: "For a change."

Brunette: "Get over it."

Baldie: "Bah."

At this point the redhead scrunched up her face — "They're always ganging up on me," she mewed — which set off further bickering between the trio. A Greek chorus minus the bodies, the drama, or an ounce of common sense.

"Say." I stepped back to appraise my partner Suzie anew. "It's like you three times over, only three times worse."

"Thanks. I think." She pursed lips. "Should I actually be thanking you at all?"

"You should. Thirty-three percent of this crap is bearable."

"Ta. What would I ever do without your compliments?"

Meanwhile the other talking heads ignored us, blathering on

about someone's hideous pair of high-heels.

"Excuse me," I cut in, to no effect.

The high-heels had been shelved in favour of a heated discussion regarding cosmetics.

"*Excuse me,*" I repeated, this time louder.

Cosmetics dovetailed into underwear — apparently the redhead's former choice of brand horrified Baldie, while Brunette tossed insults both ways.

"Oi!" Suzie suddenly yelled. Said glorious sound I never expected to hear from the kid's lungs.

All three crowns tempered the babble to stare at my partner, causing her to blush — until Brunette spoke again.

"What an uncouth young hussy."

"Agreed," Baldie said.

"Mm-hmm." That was the redhead.

"After all, she is a blonde," Brunette said.

To which Baldie agreed. "That accounts for it."

Brunette: "Check out the appalling fashion sense."

Baldie: "Rather insulting to the eye, really."

Redhead: "Urgh!"

Baldie: "And I do believe those spectacles are Pay-Less hand-me-downs."

Brunette: "No sense of pride. Look at the way she slouches."

Baldie: "Bag of bones."

Redhead: "Waste of a perfectly good body."

Brunette: "Waste of space, if you ask me."

In spite of shoddy illumination, I could see the impact these talking heads were having on Suzie. She kept eyes fastened to the floor, trusty pad dangling from a clenched left hand.

This annoyed me no end. Sure I hung crap on little Suzie Miller, but no one else was going to bite her head off within my earshot, least of all these brainpans. Easiest way to cut this torrent of abuse?

Whip out the thirty-eight.

Question was which to target. They were as bad as one another. So I spun the barrel — a feat usually impressive to those on the receiving end — and then drifted the revolver between them, only inches away from three sets of eyes.

"Heads up, ladies. I got six rounds. Two apiece."

Brunette looked less aggrieved than put out. "Oh you are droll with the bon mot. But you ought to say 'I have six rounds', dear boy, or 'I have got'. Really now."

Baldie concurred. "Clearly found his diploma in the dregs of a Weetbix packet."

Brunette let out a disdainful laugh.

My cheek twitched, mirth also the culprit, as I settled the revolver between her eyebrows. "Pick on the grammar again and you'll be picking brains off the wall — kind'a hard without fingers, you know?" I poked hard. "Well? Answer the question, dollface."

She lowered lashes. "I know."

"Swell. Now for the apology. All three of you. To my partner."

"I'm sorry," came the chorus.

Suzie smiled, readily forgiving. "Forget about it."

"Now we're all chums," I decided. "Which means we can get down to business."

Hadn't lowered the gun — I didn't feel like any more of the spoken word diarrhea, and we needed to earn our keep.

"How did your old man die?"

Baldie: "He was a useless old fool."

Brunette: "You can say that again."

Redhead: "Never amounted to anything. And couldn't get it up either."

Brunette: "Ridiculous pipe-dreams with no concept of the real world out there."

Baldie: "What a disappointment."

Redhead: "Mostly in bed."

Baldie: "A fart."

Brunette: "Completely."

Baldie: "Enough to make a girl pull one's hair out."

Brunette (glancing sideways): "That explains things."

Baldie (glaring back): "Oh, shhh."

Brunette: "You shush."

Baldie: "I could kick you — if I had legs, I mean."

Brunette: "Focus on regrowing the wig."

Baldie: "I hate you."

So much for dyking verbal nonsense. I used the gun's handle on Baldie, just a soft knock to remind her.

"Ouch!"

Straight after, Suzie leaned in to me. "Try not to break her, Roy."

"Why?"

"These are our only witnesses."

I mulled that over. "You know what? I think they're more. Tell me, ladies, did you share with Professor Jones this fine clap-trap of character assassination?"

"Of course we did," said Redhead. "We're not going to fib."

"Every day?"

"Every hour, more like it!" Brunette hissed.

"For years," added in Baldie, "so far as I'm concerned."

Brunette: "She does go back a *long* way."

Baldie: "Bitch."

Brunette: "Cow."

Regardless of the rubbish they mouthed, this made sense. "Well, congratulations, girls. Today you obviously pushed Prof Jones too far."

I placed the gun back in its holster, picked up the white sheet, and tossed it over those three irritating skulls — before reaching over to close Suze's notebook.

"Mystery solved. Hen-pecked, like I said. Let's get our pay and noodle out of here."

"Oh, droll once more," muttered one of the women from

beneath that drape. Couldn't make out which one. Didn't care.

"Let the police deal with these senseless scalps," I told Suzie as I wrapped an arm around her waist and shuffled her to the door. "C'mon. We need a head start on the cops."

Somebody else groaned, and to hell with 'em.

"She's Japanese!"

Straight after this high-pitched yelp, making the statement more a wavering question – traditional, really, for the baggage that passed herself off as my assistant – I looked at Suzie and barely flinched. Gave myself ducats for achieving that much these days.

"Which means," I said evenly, like I'd suddenly attained Zen, "something important. Am I right?"

This time round we'd stopped in a wood-paneled hallway before two closed sliding doors that were all paper and sticks. Right hand inside my jacket at the front, fingers touching the revolver. Standard practice for me, as you know, much like Suzie's whine.

"Yes, yes, yes."

Ahh, there it was. I was getting fond of the thing.

Her head barely reached my shoulders, since Suzie was stooped over and did nothing for the art of deportment. With her hands, shuffled through a wad of what she daringly labelled notes.

These were covered in a tiny biro scratching that made no sense to anyone in their right mind.

"Well?" I said. Flexed and wiggled those fingers around the Smith & Wesson.

"Ah-hah! Here we are!" The girl held aloft a single sheet, her eyes triumphant. "Yes, I was right – Japanese ghosts are definitely different."

"What, they scuttle about in kimono and clogs? Guzzle ephemeral cups of warm saké? Haunt all gruff-like, shades of Toshiro Mifune?"

"Well, I think that depends." Suzie's triumph fizzled a little. "Like whom exactly Toshiro Mifune might be."

I had to turn away. Scrutinizing flimsy doors was a far better alternative. "OK, so tell me. What're we in for once I slide back this baby?"

"Hang on a tick." More shuffling of paperwork sounded from behind.

"We can't hang here all night," I complained. Hell, now I was beginning to sound like her. My fist closed around the stock of the gun.

"We can and should if it means we get the job done properly, Roy — you know that, but you're a bully and a bull-at-the-gate, all wrapped up in one swell package."

I glanced over my shoulder, saw the kid staring at me with a glimmer of challenge there that'd mixed with remaining triumph.

"Huh." I pulled out my piece, blew out cheeks. "Alrighty then, now that's settled and in the open, let's get this sordid show on the road."

Didn't wait for more literary consultation or cross-referencing. Just went ahead and bird-dogged the behaviour she'd accused me of, kicked down the left door, and stomped into a dark living room the other side.

Suzie remained at the threshold, not so much because she hesitated but instead to examine property damage.

"Roy, d'you know how much shōji doors cost to replace?"

"Samurai always destroy them in old movies."

"Those are set-pieces."

"So the clients can take it off our bill," I muttered. Didn't really pay attention to the girl, in the middle as I was of surveying this large space surrounding us. Despite nighttime gloom I could make out a few more of those shōji-screen whatsits, a light shade that looked like a large, upside-down paper umbrella, a couple of rigid wooden chairs, and an antique secretaire. There was barely anything else.

"We can't afford any more silly deductions like this," came my assistant's berating yodel. "We're in the red as is."

"Suitable colour, given the nature of our business."

"Well, it won't be our business for long if you keep busting things."

"What can I say? I'm a bully." A second examination made me relax. The room was empty aside from skimpy Asian furnishings.

"Do you want to know now," Suzie piped up again, "exactly what we're looking for?"

"The spectre of some dead person who's a long way from home and doesn't appear to like housecalls?" The pistol returned to its holster. You can't shoot a ghost regardless.

"Not exactly." Suzie adjusted her glasses. Apparently it was difficult to read in the dark. "Says here, um, that they're called yūrei, meaning dim spirit or something."

"What, so they're not the sharpest knife in the drawer?"

"No, not 'dim' as in stupid. Not like you." The devil of a girl actually smirked. I could see that offensive thing in the half-light too. "Dim as in faint or hard to see."

"Well, ours appears to be well-nigh invisible. Does that count?"

"I don't know."

"What *do* you know?"

"Now you want to hear, after you demolished the door?"

"Not much else to do, 'less we kick back and wait for our gal."

My blonde assistant nodded to herself as she crossed the room to a window. A minor amount of streetlight allowed her to read better, most likely. I didn't know what to do in the meantime, so I squatted and laid a balancing hand atop the straw grass matting they used here.

"Apparently," my girl said, papers up round her nose, "according to Japanese custom if a person dies in a violent manner like murder, as in our subject's case, or suicide — and if they are swayed by a powerful emotion such as a desire for revenge — the yūrei has the ability to return to the physical world to seek redress."

"Fat lot of good saying 'boo' is going to do."

Now shaking her head, Suzie looked over her notes and down

at me. "If this really is an onryō, or vengeful ghost, then she's capable of causing harm in the world of the living, or even outright killing."

I held up my hand. "I have a question."

"Uh-huh?"

"Why not tell me the gruesome details before we set foot in this place."

"I was still brushing up."

"Yet now you're all groomed and coming out gloomy."

"Well, we're not in Japan. I wasn't sure if the same rules applied."

I slowly got back to my feet, pins and needles be damned. "I think they do."

"Why?" Frowning, Suzie stood straight too. "Because the dead woman was a Japanese national?"

"Possibly." I tried to swallow. Realized I couldn't. "More likely because there's a crazy-looking woman over your right shoulder, there in the corner." I nodded in that direction. Was too stricken to do more. Stared straight at this waif Suzie's height, clad in a tight white kimono, with a porcelain face peering back from beneath wild black hair. Hands, limp, hung by her sides and I couldn't seem to make out the feet.

I have no idea why, but Suzie didn't sound scared at all. "Oh, sure, OK," she chirped. "This does match the general description of your traditional onryō, even if it is a bit kabuki-fied."

"Speak English," I managed to say.

"Wouldn't it be better to try a spot of Japanese?"

"I mean make your explanations easier to understand."

"Oh."

"And I don't happen to speak the lingo. Do you?"

"No. But I brought something essential. Hang on." From the corner of my eye, still transfixed as I was by this hovering horror in the corner, I could make out Suzie searching pockets of her oversized coat. "Ah-hah!" she finally declared, producing a small book.

"Not so loud," I was straight away hissing. "You'll spook her."

"Too late for that, Roy." From the tone I sensed it was another Lame Suzie Joke That Misses Its Mark, and I'd suffered hundreds of the buggers.

"Uh-huh. Book. Tell."

"Oh! Yes." Suzie held up the tiny tome like a trophy. "The 48th printing of *Instant Japanese: A Pocketful of Useful Phrases*, first published in 1964 by Masahiro Watanabe and Kei Nagashima. It's the same one Moneypenny gives to James Bond in *You Only Live Twice*."

"Forget the pop-culture trivia, S. Use the bloody thing."

The ghost girl had patience, I'll give her that. She put up with our lopsided shenanigans, and then waited while Suzie leafed through various pages. But I didn't like the way I was ogled from beneath midnight bangs, and felt damnably chilled.

At last my blonde anchor looked up. "Kaerinasai!" she declared.

"What did you say?"

"Go home."

"I don't think that'll work."

Suzie nodded, all thoughtful like. "You're right – it's the polite version. I think we need to be more direct. Kaere!"

"Same thing?" I checked.

"Mmm-hmm. But more street-level Japanese." Inspecting the phantom on the other side of the room, Suzie shrugged. "It's not working."

"Have you ever considered the fact that we *are* in her home?"

"Well, I guess. But I meant back to purgatory or whatever, you know, in the afterlife and all that." Suddenly, Suzie tossed another phrase into the fray: "Omai, achi ike!"

"Meaning?"

"Go away."

"Yet she declines your suggestion."

"Mm-hmm."

I decided on a different approach. Anything was better than letting Suzie run the gamut of inane interpreter. Though I still couldn't move my feet, I faced our friend the yūrei/onryō. Surely the woman had lived long enough in our country to learn some local language.

"Listen, lady," I said in a voice that didn't strike me as all the confident. "It's time to move on. Your family doesn't want you hovering round, gumming up their daily lives."

The wraith lifted her head then, and I could make out dark eyes ringed with what looked like darker kohl. Who knew ghosts had makeovers?

"I was wondering when you two would address me in English," she said with better grasp of the thing than me. Sure, it came across shy and eerie but at least we'd made contact. "My Japanese isn't so great. This drove my mother to distraction, but I was brought up here."

"Oh," mumbled Suzie as she pocketed her dud solution.

Me, I decided to be more direct. We weren't on the clock with this job, and time was precious. I had whiskey sours in mind.

"OK, so the question is why exactly are you still hanging here?"

"Revenge," said the ghost.

"Uh-huh." I yawned. "Just another case of a woman scorned."

The woman shimmered in my vision. "You know, you're not very nice," she decided all by herself.

"That's what I'm always saying," agreed Suzie.

My gaze drifted between both malcontents. "Oh, hurrah. You've found a kindred spirit."

"And I'm not crazy." That was the ghost again.

"Because supernatural stalking is a clear sign of sanity." I sighed in loud fashion, the two women be damned. "Look, you might think you have a right to some kind of offbeat vendetta, but the fact is you've outstayed any welcome. We're here because your family hired us to get rid of you. I think that shows the state of things."

"Roy!" Suzie muttered.

"What?" I glanced at her. "Just telling it like it is."

Suzie then sidled up to me, to whisper in my ear. "Don't you remember what I said about this particular brand of apparition being able to exact physical harm?"

"Meh — I think the jury hadn't settled on a verdict there."

"But my notes—"

"Are theories you've filched. Show me the proof."

The yūrei/onryō or whatever she bloody well was did another of her shimmering tricks and I swear she grew a few inches in stature. The fringe-over-the-eyes trick was in full play too.

"Colour me scared," I yawned.

Which was precisely when a gust of wind stronger than I'd ever before experienced lifted me off the tatami and deposited my splayed form in a heap at the other end of this rather large room. Yeah, it hurt. I was seeing stars as I pulled myself together.

"D'you want more evidence?" Suzie asked.

"No, no. I'm fine." I pushed up against the wall, as far as possible from my assailant. "So I think we need to help you."

The ghost was in no mood for further conversation, it seemed. She was too busy looking statuesque and glowing with an eerie light.

"Suze," I decided, looking my assistant's way, "how d'we do that? Help her, I mean."

"So now you demur to my theories, Roy?"

"Better than getting lobbed about rag-doll style."

"I don't know. I'm kind of enjoying it."

"Hush, now."

"Alright, alright." She sounded more and more like me. "Simplest way? Aid her in fulfilling her purpose."

"Meaning hand over the culprit that killed her?"

"Exactly."

"Suze, the cops have no leads as to who it might be."

"Well, this is a great opportunity to quiz the victim and get some grand old come-uppance happening."

"Any other way to finish the job?"

"Uh…" The girl scanned her notes. "We don't exactly have a Buddhist priest or mountain ascetic in our office armoury, but another method is to write down holy Shintō writings that contain the name of a kami, or deity, on a piece of paper and affix this to the ghost's forehead."

I mulled over these options for all of one second. "Sounds like the priest'd be easier. And did we actually pack an adhesive?"

"Roy, get serious."

"Not easy, working with a harpy like you."

"I could leave you two to sort things out together."

"It's cool. Your harpiness has its moments."

"Is that actually a word?"

"Does it matter?"

"S'pose not." Suzie was a picture of confusion. "Should I be thanking you?"

Me? I smiled. "No need."

"Enough already!" shouted the ghost, interrupting our banter since I assumed she felt lonely. She'd also lifted toward the ceiling, I'm guessing to act more imposing. "Why on earth I returned to this mortal coil is beyond me, if I have to put up with the two of you!"

"So revenge now plays second fiddle, hmm?" I'd taken out cigarettes, but for the life of me couldn't locate the lighter. I padded down pockets with a modicum of distress.

Suzie leaned close again. "I wouldn't do that," she said.

"Why? Japanese spooks have a problem with second-hand smoke?"

"No, I mean the teasing bit. *And* this place is a tinder-trap anyway."

"Oh, God," again erupted our apparition, "please stop

talking!"

"So." I'd found the precious lighter and ignored advice. Flame reared and almost sizzled hair in my nostrils, but I ducked aside and still managed the task. Breathing in, I let the smoke linger before exhaling in loud fashion. "So, you come here on a mission to get some post curtain-call payback, but instead cop us — and haven't the nerve to deal with a dose of mind-dulling repartee. How d'you propose to deal with a cold-hearted killer?"

Ghost-girl looked down at me. Hard to tell whether the words were sinking in or she was planning to throttle yours truly. I needed an ashtray, spied a ceramic jug nearby, and surreptitiously used that.

This brought another yelp from Suzie, who'd seen the manoeuvre.

"What?" I grunted.

"I think you just ashed in this girl's cremation urn."

I looked at the jug anew. "Seriously?"

"Seriously," our phantasm confirmed on her behalf.

"Huh. Sorry." I picked up the pot, overturned it, and shook out all contents onto the matting at my feet. Yeah, there was far more than a mild-mannered two taps of a cigarette would produce, plus bonus bones. "Crap."

That was precisely when something new took place on the other side of the room from our ghost — a door slid aside to show the silhouette of a man.

"What are you doing here?" I heard him ask, even if I couldn't yet make out a face in the poor light.

"A spot of spring cleaning," I said.

"In winter?"

"Japanese style," Suzie chimed in, "like they do in Japan, before New Year."

This was news to me, but right now I was willing to go with anything. Something resembling guilt tampered with my voice box.

"Bullshit." This man, a full six inches superior to me, walked straight over and stared down at the pile of gunk on the floor. "Have you absolutely no respect for the dead?"

I realized he was either more concerned with the mess I'd made, or hadn't spotted our ethereal guest in the corner behind me.

"Death is my business," I let out in lame fashion.

That's when this guy shirt-fronted me — pushed up hard and glared down at my face. "Who are you?" he demanded. Yeah, this was a brute. One of those idiots that think they can muscle-up on people smaller in stature.

I removed the ciggie from my lips and leaned back a fraction. "Family of the deceased?"

"None of your goddamned biz." Despite imposing height his exhalation deigned to depth-charge my way and it reeked — he'd obviously been indulging in something fermented, with a tail of garlic added to the concoction and a large quantity of alcohol. The liquor made me jealous. Man could keep the rest.

"You would be the boyfriend."

This last remark came from Suzie, who spoke in an unaccustomed flat tone somewhere to the left. I couldn't check where precisely, since this hulking behemoth ran interference with my sight.

"What's it you, you four-eyed whore?"

"Um…nothing?"

"Now listen, bluster-kong," I piped up, "no one speaks like that to my assistant."

"Partner," Suzie injected.

"Partner. Same point."

"Says who?" Our newfound friend took this opportunity to lift me into the air by my shoulders, the better p'raps to see eye-to-eye.

"The bigger they are," I said. I was tired of being hefted about.

"You're the only one that'll be falling, fuckwit."

"Language, mate. There're ladies present."

He leaned right in close and personal with that pungent breath. "Your pencil-pushing bimbo? She don't count. There's no one else here."

"You sure about that?"

"Why? *You* a pussy? Seem like it, loser."

Yeah, I'd given full consideration to grabbing my gun and clocking this bastard, but wasn't happy to take another tumble when he let me go. Anyway, I didn't need to worry about the pistol since a pair of alabaster-white arms in oversized sleeves wrapped around the man's neck — apparently the wraith had shifted positions to behind him.

Our guest didn't notice. Not at first. And then his eyes began to bulge and he struggled for breath, which was when I should've realized I'd be taking a fall regardless.

Next thing I knew I was on my backside, a pain shooting up from the pointless tailbone, as big-and-smelly flailed about the room, wheezing and gasping. I watch this circus, mesmerized. The ghost, a quarter his size, slowly choked the life out of him and he was too dumb to know yet that the game was over.

Crouching beside me, Suzie placed a hand on my shoulder.

"Are you OK?" she asked, like she cared.

"Figuring I'm fine and dandy, compared to that bloke."

"I'd say he was our girl's killer."

"What gives you that fool notion?" As I spoke I glanced at my partner with what likely resembled a savage grin, if I could see it myself. "Looks like she's getting sweet revenge after all."

Suzie smiled too, resting on her haunches and blissfully oblivious to death-throes only a yard distant.

"In a minute or two we'll have fulfilled our obligations," I said. "Instead of that Shintō post-it, we ought to get a stamp made that reads 'job done'."

"I'll add it to our list. All is right in the world. A nice feeling, right, Roy?"

"Yeah." Our oversized, soon-to-be-dead paramour had collapsed face-down and twitched occasionally, with his deceased girlfriend still riding side-saddle. "I don't usually go in for gawking while a grown man carks it in a fit of supernatural mischief — but we can't save everyone."

"Exactly."

"Well, this is a first." I looked squarely at Suzie. "Have we ever agreed so much before?"

2: WAY BACK WHEN

I guess you could say the wheels fell off at sixteen.

That was when I lifted my head off the floor to peer my gut's way, at blood pumping out of a big hole in the shirtfront, running down both sides and creating a huge puddle on the carpet.

"Crap," I muttered. "That's going to be a bugger to patch."

Wasn't supposed to be like this, no way. Three days before Mitch'd reckoned it'd be a blow-over, easy-street romp — if not exactly sugar and spice and everything nice, then something marginally sweet.

The shop was down an unpopular arcade, in the city on Bourke Street, not much pedestrian traffic, and the nearest cop house three blocks away.

Basics, security-wise: a camera that probably didn't work, just for show to scare amateurs, and a newly installed magnetic tag security detector straddling the doorway. Probably bought on eBay, but we heard it go off when some kid tried something, so knew this baby was no Trojan Horse.

The bloke behind the counter seemed to actually be two people sharing the same beard, receding hairline and dress-sense (bordering on offensive suburban hippy).

There were no nametags to double-check who was who and they were always too busy reading shit to pay attention to customers' questions — which Mitch said worked to our advantage since they wouldn't know what was going on till it was too late.

The biggest attraction?

This was no diamond merchant, not a bank, nor a service station/convenience store. It wasn't even a dodgy school kiosk, our usual port-of-criminal-call.

This was a comic-book store, a minor affair specializing in new releases from America and a wad of collectibles. No manga at all, which was one of the reasons I'd never before heard of the place.

Thing was, they had a copy of *Action Comics* #1 up on the wall.

This meant nothing to me, I who coveted an early, uncensored printing of Katsura Masakazu's *Video Girl Ai* manga, since later printings changed the art to cover up the nudity.

Mitch courteously filled in the massive gaps in my American comic knowhow: *Action Comics* #1 gave Superman his big debut, published in the U.S. in 1938 for just ten cents. Over seventy years later a rare copy was sold online for $2.16m.

"You know Nick Ratatouille?" Mitch went on.

"Maybe." I'd been out front of the folks' place, sitting on my bum on the nature-strip fixing an elusive puncture in the tyre of a painstakingly rebuilt 1974 Malvern Star chopper, trying not to get tangled up in Mitch's plans.

Mitch had a tendency to lead partners astray — namely arrest or injury, or both — even if he always got off scot-free. Still, this was one question I believed I could tackle without a lure or a slap. "Isn't he the muscle for Occitan and the boys over on Catalan Crescent?"

"Right on. He heard from a mate who heard from another mate that it was sold by Nicolas Cage."

"You reckon the comic in that shop is the same one once owned by him?"

"No, you moron — but if that one got two mill, there's every chance the one on the wall in this dive will get half that, at least. A million, R, that we can split down the middle. You could get your bloody Malvern Star gold-plated if you want."

That'd been the clincher. Not the gold plating but the swandooly.

So I went along with it all, even forking out the dosh for the ski masks from an army disposals shop on Elizabeth Street and a couple of BB-guns I got FedEx'd from Japan that were replica full-scale Enfield revolvers.

Knocking over a comic-book store would be a breeze. Nothing could go wrong.

We'd skipped high school on a Monday — had forged the

letters from our mums as usual — and got out of uniforms in the toilets at South Yarra Station before heading into town on a Frankston Line train at 2:10 p.m.

Got off at Flinders Street before three, after typical bloody delays, and waltzed straight to the arcade. Flicked through some brand new Marvel comics that bored me silly, waiting till no one else was in the shop, and then pulled on the balaclavas and pointed our faux firearms at the bird behind the counter.

"Give us the fucking comic, dickhead!" Mitch screamed in too loud a voice.

"Sure, kid, sure, don't get your knickers in a knot," old Beard-and-Bald assured him, hands clutching air. "Which one?"

"Clark Kent up there, on the wall." Mitch waved the gun in a general direction over the clerk's head. "Move it!"

"You mean... Are you talking about this?" The man pointed to *Action Comics* #1, showing a primitive Superman lifting a green car above his head and smashing it.

"Sure. Hand-pass it over."

"You boys do realize it's a repro?"

I leaned forward. "A what?"

"Reproduction. This isn't the real thing — why on earth would we have it sitting right here in our shop? That'd be lunacy."

I couldn't be sure, but sussed the old hippy was lying. Mitch, however, was in a rage, shoving his popgun forward.

"Bullshit!" he shouted, so incensed he lost control of his drool.

I observed this spittle traveling across air from my partner's mouth; saw it settle down on the desktop and sit there, bubbly and offensive.

That was when Beard-and-Bald got angry. He stared at the saliva, and then dropped his right hand—fretting some, Mitch waggled his toy, shouting "Don't move!"—and in reply the man stood up straight with an Uzi submachine gun stuck in his mitt. Me? I had a sneaking suspicion this baby hadn't been purchased via mail order from Tokyo; conjecture confirmed when the thing start dishing out real 9mm bullets.

"Nobody spits in my shop! No fucker steals my comics!" Beard-and-Bald raved as he raked the small area, destroying much of the merchandise before he found his real targets.

Mitch, I could see from my place spread-eagled on my back, was dead as a dodo, folded up against the wall with brains wallpapering a bunch of DC comics in a rack.

Returning attention to my stomach, I felt dizzy, tried to pull together the flaps of skin there — same technique as sticking together the flaps of rubber with the puncture the other day.

Now, if only I'd had my tyre-sealant glue.

After I got released from hospital a few weeks later we had court-hearings to worry about and I talked up dropping out of school. My parents wouldn't have a bar of it. Trouble was, since I was sixteen I could be tried as an adult. While Dad raved on re: medical and legal expenses, all I could think was that they were lucky they didn't have to fork out dosh for a funeral like Mitch's oldies did. I ended up selling the Malvern Star to some collector via The Trading Post but it barely made a dent in the bills.

I remember Beard-and-Bald made the *Melbourne Times* as a local shop store hero with his Travis Bickle routine just as the worms'd started burrowing into my mate's brow.

There was a photo of him touting that Uzi, with a debonair grin on his face.

Funnily enough, I never stood trial.

One of Dad's besties, a man I'd known since I was a kid, had pull with the law and somehow one-upped the legal system so that the case was quietly dropped. The payback was that he'd become my legal guardian, a kind of ad-hoc parole type I'd have to report to three times a week after school.

His name was Art Miller, and he decided that what this amounted to was a good opportunity to indulge in slave labour. For several hours every Monday and Wednesday evening, and all day Saturdays, I'd have to do a lot of trivial crap for him in his office at 1924 North Wilcox Avenue.

This office thankfully comprised of just two rooms, a dumpy pair of boxes in a dump of a block that hadn't been renovated or upgraded since art deco was de rigueur.

One room was some kind of reception cubicle about four by four, boasting a bench seat with patched-up leather upholstery and nothing else.

This led to the office-proper which was only a couple of feet larger.

Art was some kind of P.I. or snoop and I'd swear he hadn't tidied his workplace in the last decade. One of my jobs was cleaning up ten years' worth of gunk. I ripped up a carpet that had become its own thriving domain of bacterial growth, threw out a coffee maker that had fungus climbing out the back, and bleached the hell out of his collection of sordid-looking, mostly chipped porcelain.

Furnishings wise there was an ancient wooden desk over by the single window, which had a busted venetian blind pulled up to reveal a lovely view of a wall a few feet distant, and we had a lamp. There were a couple of uncomfortable armchairs either side of the desk. Next to the window sill a calendar hung at an angle no matter how many times you tried to straighten it. The place had little else to make things cozy: a few books, pictures, radio, chessmen, old letters, and other meaningless rubbish like that. There was a worse-for-wear cassette of Tom Waits' album *Small Change* that had the tape spilling out.

A narrow bookcase with four shelves stood to the right of the desk, mostly packed with mint-condition, yawn-inspiring tomes on jurisprudence — for show, I think — as well as a collection of genuinely worn-out novels by Dashiell Hammett, Raymond Chandler and Mickey Spillane.

On top of this was the only photo, Art's daughter Suzie in primary-school uniform, smiling from behind over-large spectacles. Her mother's arm was apparent in the left corner of the portrait but the woman had been cut out — likely after my boss got his divorce.

Not long after I started serfdom I found my employer had an apparently illegal gun in the middle draw of his desk — no BB, this — and it also had a layer of grime on it. In the left-hand desk drawer was a bourbon bottle that changed labels and content amounts but never had any dust.

Another chore was organizing a filing system for clients and accounts that had less order to it than Imelda Marcos's footwear collection.

Still, I ended up flicking through much of this mishandled

paperwork. It became clear that Art's main clientele came from other people's equally messy divorce cases, along with stalking claimants on behalf of the Transport Accident Commission to see if he couldn't get surveillance footage of whiplash victims doing aerobics.

The workload had steadily decreased over the past couple of years while restaurant and bar bills ran in the opposite direction. Clearly Art's raging alcoholism and propensity for illegal pharmaceuticals hadn't helped.

Two years later I somehow graduated from high school and ended up in an arts course at uni where I wasn't seriously expected to bone-up on cinema studies in any way other than watching old films — which I dug anyway — so my penance with that other kind of Art increased to five evenings a week, as well as Saturday from 10 a.m. to 5 p.m.

Given that my boss rarely showed himself in the office before two in the afternoon, this meant I had about four hours to myself and I had the pretense-of-working angle down pat.

So it was that I hugged the curve of the desk, partially playing sham detective but more honestly hungover and bored out of my brain, when a dame came to call — unannounced, as the choice ones usually do.

And this, dear reader, is my intentional play on words. The woman had no choice.

Fact was my employer not only underpaid me but also refused to invest in a receptionist, and this accounted for the reason our visitor wandered in with an addled expression stuck on her mush. I sat up straight to wave, before contemplating how stupid this also looked.

If she noticed, the woman let me off any hook. She indicated our only other chair on her side of the bureau, ironing-board posture putting mine to shame.

"May I?"

"Sure."

A young one, maybe late teens sliding into early twenties. Had long, golden-brown hair severely tied back in a way that framed a beautiful face with minimal makeup. I noticed her eyes mugged the colour of cinnamon.

To balance this and likely buck unwanted attention, the woman wore an abstract floral dress looking like Claude Monet and Jackson Pollock painted it in wild collusion.

"Are you Mister Miller?" she said as my eyes adjusted to the glare.

"Sorry, he's out. My shift."

"I see. I'm Mocha Stockholm."

"Course you are."

The woman frowned, though on that face said expression barely made a dent. "You know me?"

"Nah. Just sounded like a quip Humphrey Bogart would've rolled out — with far more panache, I'll give you that."

"To which, Lauren Bacall would be duty-bound to lob back her own face-slapping wisecrack?"

"The devil, you say...?" I broke out in a grin. "You know your classic cinema."

"A wee bit. My mum was a movie journalist, so I grew up force-fed on the stuff. She particularly loved her black-and-white detective stories, Mister—?"

"Scherer."

"Mister Scherer."

"Call me Roy."

"Roy, then." She smiled. We looked at each other for several seconds. "Care to know why I've come today, Roy?"

"Oh, yeah, 'course — sorry."

I grabbed a notebook, and the first biro I scribbled with refused to work. I rifled through the top desk drawer, avoiding the one beneath with the pistol, as I searched for another.

"Would you mind if I smoke?" I heard the woman say while I ransacked the bureau. What was her handle? Москва? Better to stick with the family name.

"No worries, Miss Stockholm."

"Mocha."

"Mocha. Sure — so long as you don't mind sharing one of the cigarette's brothers. I'm out."

Mocha pulled her chair closer.

As she renounced good deportment to recline back into it, the woman crossed a pair of obscenely long, narrow legs. I hadn't noticed before the minimal length of her overwrought dress.

She conjured up an ostrich-skin-covered cigarette case and slipped out two ciggies.

"Help yourself."

Case in hand, Mocha leaned over and I prized one free. I tried my urbane best to snap up the fag with style, but my mitt shook. That'd be the excessive amount of cognac, consumed the prior evening, revealing itself.

The woman lit our cigarettes with a Zippo that had the slogan *La Chauve-souris* inscribed in a flowing font across its surface.

Settling back to enjoy the moment I sensed the return of a wayward backbone, and granted my guest a grateful smile. She'd earned the truth.

"I have a confession," I said. "I'm not really a detective, just hired help."

"I suspected as much."

Mocha held the cigarette between her teeth as she placed the case and lighter into a small purse, and then she took it in her left hand.

"There's only one name on the business card — Mister Miller's. You're also a little young."

"No younger than you."

She pursed lips, but there was a smirk there. "Too young to play the hardened, streetwise P.I. You need to get out in the sun more often, weather-up the good-looks."

"You're a better detective than me."

"Something I always aspired to. Let me guess: part-time job?"

"Bingo. Pays the bills and saves me scabbing off my parents." Debts and prior indiscretions didn't need to be iterated here.

"They object?"

"To the scabbing? I do."

The woman nodded, but I noticed she was looking over at the tattered venetian blind I'd closed to fend off an offensive midday sun that somehow conspired to work its way between buildings.

"The odd-jobs you do here. Surveillance, that sort of thing?"

"Would be neat-o if true. Alas, nada. Mostly paper shuffling and photocopy chores. I double-up as a cleaner, barman and short-order cook. I'm quite the whiz with an egg, a shaker, and a pot of boiling water. But I don't think Art trusts me at this point in the field to do real things like surveillance."

"Art would be Mister Miller?"

"Yep."

With her free hand, Mocha pulled at the hem of her dress, which was riding too high on killer thighs. I praised my lucky stars that Art had never invested in a wider desk.

"Speaking of whom," the woman murmured, "can I ask where he is? We had an appointment for twelve."

"That so?"

Mocha gifted me a laugh. "That *is* so."

This was a potential problem.

Art had been on the receiving end of most of that cognac the night before — two bottles of Château de Plassac, an undeserved gift from some unusually grateful client. I'd drunk maybe half of one of them, Art the rest. Plus he'd snorted a couple of lines of speed to my single. Given the current state of my brain, I assessed he'd be sleeping the cocktail off right into the next week.

I therefore pretended to check a $2-shop desk calendar my boss never used. "Stockholm," I mused, feigning diligence. "Named after the city?"

"No, silly — the city's named after me."

"Right." I looked up at the woman. "He's — um — indisposed right now, out on a case, but give me the details and I'll fill him in."

"Have you found a pen that works?"

"Right here."

I was holding aloft a gaudy biro with cute images of Minnie Mouse splashed all over the thing. Where the blazes had Art acquired that?

"Fine." The woman gave me a pleasant enough smile — difficult to read. "I think someone is trying to kill me."

I'd just crossed the t in 'think' — shorthand wasn't my forté — when she finished talking. The comment hung in the air like a predatory slap about to happen. I looked at her under my brow.

"You think...?"

Mocha glanced at the pad beneath my pen. "I think someone is trying to kill me."

"I know — you said."

"Well, you haven't finished writing."

"I'm not sure I need to — easy enough to remember."

I took one last drag on my cigarette, which was already burning at the filter.

"What I meant to ask is this: You *think* someone is trying to kill you, or you have actual proof?"

"Well, I have these. See what you make of them."

Mocha had popped open her handbag — this was a Prada, but I had no idea if counterfeit or real — and she took out a handful of twice-folded beige envelopes that were placed on the desk within easy reach. I picked them up and counted. Five in all, no address or postage stamp — just Mocha's name typed on the front.

"They were slipped under the door of my apartment," she said. "Well, four were put there. The fifth I discovered in my locker at the theatre."

"You're an actress?"

"Ballet dancer."

The perfect comportment of her legs crossed my mind. I opened the flap of one of the envelopes and unfolded an abnormally large page.

Mocha leaned forward to place elbows on top of Art's ink blotter map of the world, her chin in her palms. "It's U.S. Letter, eight-point-five by eleven inches."

"You measured it?"

"Like you, obviously, I thought this was a weird size. I checked into it. Whereas we use the international standard A4, U.S. Letter is the standard in—"

"The U.S.?" I hazarded.

"Spot on."

"Ta. Wasn't that difficult."

"Names are not always a giveaway. Think about French fries."

"True." I turned attention to the contents. "Let's see now: 'YOU WILL DIE!!' ...To the point, all caps, double exclamation

47

marks for effect — making the threat childish. Not so sure of him or herself, since 'WILL' is employed instead of 'GOING TO'. Wow. You're right. This *is* a threat."

"Using a manual typewriter."

"Manual?" I stared closer at the print. "Old-school. Scrub the childish quip. And looks like the 'L' drops down lower than the other keys."

Mocha narrowed eyes as she reviewed the page. Straight after I had to shake my head to clear it of the vision. The woman's peepers were dazzling.

"I hadn't noticed that," she was saying.

"Mmm." I flicked through other envelopes in my hands. "All these letters are written with the same machine?"

"I'm fairly certain, yes."

"Similar commentary?"

"Pretty much. Things like 'Die, bitch', 'Prepare to meet your maker' — et cetera, et cetera. I haven't learned all of them by rote."

"Original content."

"Requiring writerly skill and excessive imagination."

"For sure. Any idea why some dipstick would want you bumped off?"

"I haven't the faintest." Straight after she lifted her head from her hands. "Actually, that's not exactly true. I was recently promoted to principal."

"Of which school?"

Mocha rolled those mesmerizing cinnamon eyes. "I'm nineteen. A little young to be a teacher, let alone running a school. I meant principal dancer at the company — what the French call *étoile*."

"Well, I'm glad we got that sorted out early," I laughed.

She charitably joined in. "That's true. Could have led to a disastrous misunderstanding."

"Oh, yeah. Now, back to the manual typewriter." Balancing

the chair on its two back legs — which my boss hated me doing — I scratched my head. "Prob'ly easy enough to find in this day and age. What a giveaway."

"Then you'll take the case?"

"I'll have to run it by Art when he steps in. Guy's a busy man."

"Not your Mister Miller — you. Will you take the case?"

I stared at her. "Me?"

"I like the way you think, even while you're nursing what I can only imagine is the hangover from Hades."

"You noticed."

"Mmm. But I think we have something, a spark. I trust you, in spite of any — er — alcoholic tendencies."

"Well, I'm not qualified anyway. No detective am I. Art runs the show and he'd hit the roof."

"I don't care. Qualifications are often a ruse or no help at all. I'll pay well — and throw in a few front-row tickets."

"You have that kind of pull?" I guessed it must be a third-rate affair, probably some amateur collective doing rehearsals in a dilapidated warehouse on a back alley in Richmond or Clifton Hill.

"Right now, I seem to."

"Which company?"

"The national one."

"Ah." I seriously needed to reassess my detecting skills. "Big time."

"These days, with the world falling apart out there — I guess."

"Sorry to say, I'm not such a ballet fan, so the tickets would be a wasted perk."

"Any sisters?"

That made me twig. Art's kid Suzie.

I could imagine her killing for the tickets — or, better yet, strangling me if I passed up this kind of opportunity. A tough ten-year-old mad about ballet. I peered at my watch. God knows why. The old man wouldn't be back for days and, anyway, he wouldn't notice I was MIA.

"Okay," I decided. "You're on."

We entered the Arts Centre complex via a back door that reminded me of hidden panels used by ninja in old Japanese TV shows.

I didn't even see it there in the wall till Mocha stopped to swing the thing open. Just as I stepped forward, another skinny woman — coming from inside — whacked into my guide.

The glare this woman sent Mocha's way bookended the intentional nature of said bump. I would have guessed her age as early thirties, with crow's feet round the eyes and a boyish body she didn't hide. Pretty woman, yet washed out and agitated.

"I see you're replacing me in the part," this woman said.

Mocha held ground. "It's just temporary."

"Of course. Nobody here is a permanent fixture."

After this oddball exchange, the woman waltzed on down the street. I'll give her this much — she waltzed well.

"Who's grumpy bum?" I asked.

"Neve Ryan."

"And the name is supposed to be meaningful to me, because...?"

"The darling of the company over the past decade — but she's being forced into retirement by our new director Murray Helpman."

"Bound to make someone grumpy. Any chance, you reckon, she could be the author of your fan mail?"

"Well, Neve doesn't like me."

"I don't like people, either — but that doesn't mean I send irate love letters or plan to knock them off."

"True. C'mon."

I followed the woman's lead along a narrow corridor wrapped

in pale linoleum and very little else aside from intrusive fluorescent lighting above our heads.

"So this is Ballet Central?"

"The bowels of it."

Near an open door a wiry-looking middle-aged man in baggy chocolate-brown pyjamas, boasting a beige cravat around the neck and thinning hair up on top, intercepted us. He had this somewhat magnetic ski-jump nose undercut by a lopsided sneer.

"Darling," the gent purred, ignoring me while he washed bulging eyes over Mocha. "Where on earth have you been?"

"Lunch with my friend Roy here. Roy, this is Murray Helpman — the artistic director of the company."

"Yes, yes, charmed," Helpman crooned, allowing his gaze to flick my way for all of one five hundredth of a second. "Now—" His attention had jumped back to Mocha "—I want to create, to make something big out of something little, to make a great dancer out of you. But first, I must ask you a question: What do you want from life? To eat?"

The man appeared genuinely disgusted at the thought.

"Don't worry, I threw down only a salad," Mocha assured him.

"And didn't throw it back up," I added. "Even with a liberal dashing of Thousand Island dressing."

Helpman fairly swooned. The man leaned against a wall, wiping his brow with a floral hanky. "Oh, my God! Insanity!"

"Roy's only kidding," Mocha said, granting me a look that was thirty-three percent annoyed and the other two-thirds mischief. "No Thousand Island dressing, I swear."

Another man, handsome, taller and more powerful-looking than Helpman, strode up to us in a pair of white tights and a loose black T-shirt with the word 'IF?' emblazoned across the chest.

"What is this I hear for Thousand Island dressing? I love the Thousand Islands!"

"Oh, Bruno, shush."

Mocha now seemed disproportionately annoyed. It was a sad thing to see the mischief scarper.

"Roy, this is my dance partner, Bruno Lermentov. He's from Slobokia."

I glanced at the man. "Is that a real country?"

"Ahh, of course, of course! Very nice to meet you, Mister Roy." Bruno was all odd eastern European twang, shaking my hand with a strong grip that made my bones creak. Then he leaned in close, glittery eyes holding mine from beneath a brunette fringe. "Am I not magnificent?"

"Sorry. It's a bit of a madhouse."

We'd entrenched ourselves in a large dressing room that Mocha had scored for herself. It even had her name on the door — my dream.

One wall was naked brickwork, while opposite a huge mirror sat above a dresser. Light bulbs surrounded the looking glass and a clothesline dangled across just above head-height, holding an assortment of undergarments and jewellery.

Below, the dresser was jammed with powders, creams, rouge, lipsticks, brushes and other bric-à-brac I had no hope of recognizing.

"D'you mean it's a madhouse right here or the ballet company in general?"

"Both?" Mocha giggled.

I barely recognized the woman.

She'd changed into a sequined leotard with a wide, frilly tutu, while on the face she'd slapped a thick layer of white greasepaint, black eyeliner and ridiculously long false lashes. An ostrich-feather headpiece up top set it all off. Her midriff above the tutu was bare — a narrow, muscled thing that had absolutely no excess puppy fat. This was difficult to keep my hands away from.

At that particular moment Mocha was grinding her feet in a small wooden box on the ground.

"Kitty litter?" I asked from my crap fold-up captain's chair by the door.

"Ha-Ha. No. This is ballet rosin, a powder resin we rub our toes and heels in to avoid slippage."

"Oh, I get it — a fancy version of the blue chalk we use on billiard cues for a game of pool."

"Mm-hmm."

Wasn't sure what she meant by her tone there.

"Anyway, I have a performance now. I've reserved a seat for you in the wings." She stepped out of the tray and pushed a ticket into my hand. "I'll see you after?"

"Sure. Might do a spot of snooping."

"Well, if you're also hungry —you'll have to pop out for something. There's a half-decent restaurant next door called The Archers, so try that. None of the other dancers have anything except rabbit food, and since he took over I'm certain Murray is trying to starve us all to death."

"How long's he been in charge?"

"Two months, ever since Pat Hingle's terrible accident."

"In what way terrible?"

"She was found in the loo — disemboweled, stabbed multiple times, and hung from a doorframe with her own tights."

"You call that an accident?"

"The police did. Anyway, I can't complain. Pat tended to ignore me, but once Murray took over he gave me the promotion."

The woman placed her arms in an 'L' position — the left one out straight beside her, the right pointed my way, and then she pirouetted on one leg several times, so swiftly her body became a blur. When she finished the rotation she struck a pose with her arms crossed low in front and one foot forward.

"*Bras Croisé*," she announced.

I couldn't help myself — I gave a healthy round of applause.

Mocha winked at me. "Warm up." Her gaze whipped over to a digital clock half hidden behind paraphernalia on that crowded makeup stand. "Gotta go, Roy — duty calls. Ciao!"

About three hours later, after countless curtain calls, once the orchestra had packed up and the audience piled out, Mocha came to find me in the right wing seats. She was still dolled-up, but had wrapped herself in a bland, cream woolen cardigan and had ostrich feathers at a jaunty angle. Surprisingly her makeup had held together okay. Looking sweaty as she did, the complete package came across sexy.

"So — what did you think of *Le Corsaire*?" she said as she flopped next to me and stuck her pointe shoes on the chair in front. "I presumed you might enjoy it since there're pirates tucked away in the faintly ridiculous plot."

I glanced at her. "Honest answer?"

"Go on."

"I dozed through most of it."

"And I thought you were supposed to be keeping an eye on me."

"I had my leftie half-open."

"Does that count?"

"In my book, yep. Quite the struggle."

"Did you find any typewriters?"

"Forgot to bring my magnifying glass. Bring me up to speed on the yarn behind the ballet."

"There isn't one. Remember I said it was faintly ridiculous?"

"You're kidding."

"It's the performance that matters. Kind of."

"Right." I rubbed my face and peered around an empty auditorium. "Big place. How many people does it hold?"

"A thousand at capacity."

"How many were here today."

"A thousand."

Mocha stood then and took my hand, which surprised me. I allowed her to lead me away from the comfy chair to a small set of stairs, and then up onto the stage.

Some of the spots high above still glowed, but the arena and its ramshackle sets created a dark forest effect that looked vaguely menacing — in a wire clothes hanger and papier-mâché way.

"Don't you get stage-fright in front of all those gawking plebs out there?"

"Sometimes my heart is in my stomach. Other times, I don't care. They're going to be building a larger theatre next door — it'll hold five times as many people, apparently. *That's* scary."

"Ballet that popular?"

"Didn't think so, but I don't make these decisions. An audience of five thousand is too big — can you see the dancers at all from the back pews? Next up, they'll erect video screens in the rear for those people — which means they might as well save their money and enjoy the spectacle on a telly at home."

I decided on the spot the girl was cute when she soapboxed.

"How long've you been prancing chums with Bruno the Magnificent?"

"Ouch." Mocha slid off the humdrum cardigan and watched it fall to the boards. "You make us sound like some kind of glitzy ballroom dancing duo."

"Never."

"Huh. We've been together a month, since I was elevated to principal. Bruno was Neve's partner before that."

"Bound to make waves."

"A drop in the ocean." Mocha smiled.

"So, no death notes in your locker this arvo?"

"Nothing. But we've only been here half a day. Rome wasn't built in twice that."

"Neither was my attention span. How long did it really take to build Rome?"

"I don't remember them teaching us — we learned only the idiom."

"That figures."

I gazed up at the pulleys and ropes, lights and wire several dozen metres above, at the same time that I stretched the muscles in my back. Slouching felt way too conspicuous in these parts.

"Before you became a principal, you were one of those background people?"

"A member of the *corps de ballet*? Yep."

"What's the wire on them? Any grumpsters among that lot?"

"People annoyed by my promotion? I don't know. Haven't thought to take a survey." Perhaps feeling guilty, the girl picked up her cardigan to hang it on a small faux rock.

"When were you upped to prima?"

"Five weeks ago."

"When did the fan mail begin?"

"Five weeks ago."

I looked at her. "The exact same day you were promoted?"

"Yep — that was the night I received the one in the locker. After that they've been hand-delivered by the arsehole to my apartment."

"Before, or after, the announcement?"

"Which one?" Mocha was confused.

"The announcement about your upgrade — promotion."

"God, I don't know. It was ages ago."

"Try to remember."

Mocha frowned and her eyes darted about as she searched memory. It seemed to be a losing battle, but then the girl parted her cherry-red lips and stared at me.

"Before? Crap — yes. You're right. It *was* before. We had a matinée performance of *The Sleeping Beauty*. Neve was Aurora, Bruno the Prince and I was the Lilac Fairy. Neve was so beautiful, Roy. I'd never, ever seen anyone dance Aurora so—"

I cleared my throat. "The letter, Mocha."

"Hmm?"

"The letter in the locker."

"Oh! Yes, sorry. After the performance ended I brushed out my hair, had a shower, got changed to go to the company fundraiser upstairs that evening — that was where the announcement about my promotion was to be made. I found the letter beforehand, squeezed into my locker through the grille."

"You weren't concerned?"

"Didn't take the thing seriously, I wasn't sure if it was a joke or some silly stalker's handiwork. No time to fret."

"Who knew you were being promoted?"

I was thinking of either Bruno the Magnificent or Neve, the forced retiree.

Incriminating ballet shoes best fit the two of them. Frankly, nothing would've made me happier than to pin the wrong number tag on the guy who'd crushed my fingers — they still ached.

"Did Bruno or Neve know about it?" I added.

"No. Well, I'm pretty sure no. Even I didn't know until the announcement was made. I spotted Neve's face straight after — she was horrified, but she also looked shocked. The woman played a wonderful Aurora, but she's not that great an actress."

"Bruno?"

"Off chasing tutu. He'd slipped out straight after the encore to catch a flight to Sydney. Some dancer up there he has his hands all over."

I breathed out loudly and looked around. We were alone. I never realized a theatre could be so eerie when no one was in it.

"When is this place closed up for the night?"

"They'll be switching off the lights in an hour or two."

"Do they object to people hanging round like we are now?"

"Usually it's okay."

"So security is lax. People come, people go."

"I never gave it much thought. Yes."

After testing its stability I sat down on a prop representing an anchor. "The key is the typewriter, but I doubt we'll find that here. You'd hear a manual a mile off."

"We can't exactly ransack people's homes."

"Who says? Art does it all the time."

"And you?"

"The only ransacking I ever did was my older brother's room, looking for his chocolate stash."

"He had one?"

"Stolen from the school tuckshop."

I performed the usual head scratch I'd picked up second hand from Art.

"Let's go back a way. Who would've known before the announcement? Who decides these things? — And had the time to whiz home, type up a missive on their fancy antique machine that probably needed to be oiled-down beforehand, and then get back here — all this before the party — to make a letter drop?"

Same moment, we glanced at one another.

Helpman.

Straight after this amateur deduction I was seeing stars.

Something damnably hard had hammered me from behind, across the back of the skull, knocking me right off the anchor. I lay face down on the stage. The pain was excruciating and I thought I'd pass out — but didn't. Held on for dear life, since I knew life was probably something give-or-take right then.

Took a while to pull myself to hands and knees, idiotic notions of protecting Mocha flying bat-crazy across my senses. Had to wait longer still to clearly see clearly.

When I finally did, I found a sprinkling of blood on the floor-boards — mine? Mocha's?

Velveteen stage curtains hung nearby so I used them to pull myself up. I felt woozy and things threatened to bank sideways, but at least they'd stopped spinning.

Bruno the Magnificent stood a few metres away, at the edge of the orchestra pit, a glassy look on his face as he watched me totter.

"You?" I managed.

The dancer peered down at his right hand.

There was an iron weight in his fingers, something heavy enough to have been the object that whacked me — and, in fact, there was hair and a tuft of scalp attached to it, but the hair was the wrong colour.

It was black instead of my brown.

A thick spilling of blood from his hairline coursed down the Slobokian's face.

"It fell on my head, yet!" he declared of the metal, holding it aloft for conjecture, and then he toppled sideways with a loud thud.

I could tell he was dead the moment the echo faded.

"A wonderful dancer — but in all other respects a cretin."

The theatre director, Helpman, came around a towering prop of a pirate ship the anchor belonged to. This newcomer kicked Bruno's body and he smiled.

"All that gutter English and poorly pronounced mumbo-jumbo. Perhaps I really ought to have bludgeoned him earlier."

"Then *you're* the one that slugged me."

"Naturally."

"Don't see what's natural about that," I muttered. "Where's Mocha?"

I didn't have time to hear any reply. My skull puttered and I again fell to my knees. Yes, concern had come home to bat and I also realized I had to play for time —at the current moment I was in no state to put up a half-decent fight.

So, yeah, time. I needed some of that for a miracle to happen.

"Oh, and what a fine question that is," Helpman was nattering now — like all good villains should, wasting precious seconds. "I thought she was with you. Where *has* the girl got to?"

The man glanced about, displaying a relatively minor sense of unease.

If Mocha'd taken a powder, good for her. Less to worry about. But I still needed the time I talked up, and a smidgeon of clarity — p'raps I could even convince him to tip his mitt, for all the good that'd do me. Curiosity always was one of my weak points, alongside bailing-up comic-book stores with fake handguns.

"Can I ask you something?" I said.

"This depends, does it not?"

"Really? On what?"

"On the question, of course."

"Well, okay, whatever. Yeah — I guess." Shook my head. Vision was blurring again, but I kept to the chase like Art used to tell me about when he watched me like a hawk making his favourite mixed drinks. "Anyway, um — d'you happen to have a typewriter?"

"A typewriter?"

"A manual one."

"As a matter of fact, I do. A gift from my father."

"Does it get stuck?"

"Eh?"

"On its 'L's? Do the keys sometimes get stuck on the L?"

"Ahh. I see where you're taking this, Roger."

"Roy."

"I don't think your name is something you need to worry about ever again."

"Seriously?"

"Very seriously."

"Yeah, yeah, OK, I get that. But one thing I don't get — you're the one who sent Mocha those crazy notes."

"Hands up, all guilty parties!" Helpman raised the five fingers of his left hand into the air and laughed in an unnerving kind of way.

"You're real hysterical, mate. So...why? You promoted Mocha

to principal ballerina."

That killed the merriment.

"*Dancer*. Good Lord, nobody says 'ballerina' anymore."

"Dancer. Same question."

Helpman raised both arms now, outstretching them toward the empty seats of the theatre. "Great agony of body and spirit can only be achieved by a great impression of simplicity!" he announced with a booming voice — either clearly mad, or up for a slice of ham acting.

As I studied the palooka I felt more than a little confused, and pretty certain this wasn't concussion-related.

"I think you want to word that the other way round, mate," I decided.

"Who, pray tell, is the artistic director here?"

"Doubt you are. You strike me as more the professional nut-job."

"Oh, ho!" Helpman chuckled without mirth. "Do get these giddy observations off your chest before I crack that head wide open."

"Nah. I've got a better idea."

"Is that so?"

Time was working its wee little magic. I could see better and the noggin didn't feel like it had quite so many trolls tap-dancing about.

"Yeah, I do — let's bite the bullet, here and now. You're going to kill me, so let's be upfront. I'm Roy Scherer and I work for a detective agency. The training wheels still haven't been detached, but there you go. I live in a mate's apartment, sleeping on his couch, and I have no money in the bank. My sad story in a nutshell. But Art Miller, my boss, knows I'm here and you won't want to mess with him."

The speech made me giddy. I wiped the back of my head, finding wetness there. When I put the hand in front of my face, it was covered with sticky red blood. I blinked a few times, feeling ill.

"Now you," I said in a small voice. "What's your real moniker? I know Helpman is a sham."

"Do you now?"

"Sure," I lied.

"And why would I bother going into such detail?"

"I think a better question is why not?"

He smiled then. "Pathetic. All right. My name is Ivan Boleslawsky."

"OK. Never remember that. And your caper?"

"If you're asking me what this is all about, you'd be better off directing the question to Mocha's mother. Mocha? Oh, Mocha?"

The man turned full circle on the stage, looking about for our girl.

"Where the devil has she got to? The silly fool can't escape. I locked all the doors, and the keys are right here." He tapped the breast pocket of his blazer.

Felt again like I was going to pass out. Not yet.

"Go on," I urged.

"Hmm?" The man stopped searching. "Oh yes, of course, the story! Are you sure you want to hear this?"

"Love to."

"Well, many years ago, Mocha's mother — a hack journalist, I must say — wrote a review of my father's film. Do you know the famous Ruritanian director Rudolf Boleslawsky?"

"Nope."

"There's a tragedy. A great man. His dramatic style was sublime, bordering on cinéma vérité, a moving, and—"

"You talked up a critique."

"Oh, yes. So I did. Thank you. This film 'review' was first published in *The Age* newspaper here in Melbourne. That would have been damaging enough, but the harpy syndicated the piece to *The Independent* in England and *The New York Times* in America. It even appeared in the esteemed *Ruritanian Gazette*. That five hundred-word missive destroyed my father's career and broke his heart — a year later he tried to drown my mother in the kitchen sink, and he was then committed to a mental institution. I was sixteen years old. A humiliating experience."

"For your dad or for yourself?"

"Myself, of course."

I worked my jaw and produced a yawn of some standing. "Y'know, this yarn is about as interesting as the story behind *Le Corsaire*."

The man's eyes bulged. "How dare you!" he hissed.

Straight after Bole-whatever-his-name-was strode over to Bruno's corpse to snatch up that iron weight from the dead man's fingers.

"Now — now I'm going to return the favour by killing not just that evil reporter's only child, but her rude, highly unprofessional prick of a bodyguard."

"Looks like my luck's run out then."

"Bad luck isn't brought by broken mirrors, but by broken shoes. Remember that."

I glanced up at him and his gleaming club. "That doesn't even make sense."

"Young man, why would you look a gift-horse in the mouth?"

"What's the point? You're going to crown me anyway."

"True."

The kook stepped toward me then. I still had to hold tightly to the curtains and therefore couldn't raise hands to defend myself.

"Modern man is so confused, Robert," he nattered on.

"Roy."

"I do stand corrected. But it's much better to work in the theatre — than in the horror of a world out there."

"Whatever. Just hit me and get this over with."

That was when all hell really broke loose.

Something fast darted out of the shadows of a mocked-up

grotto to my right, moving so quickly I couldn't hope to keep a bead on it. Don't know when I realized the wildly whirling dervish was Mocha.

She hummed something familiar as she zipped, twisted, did a cartwheel — what was that damned tune? — and then finally somersaulted, catapulted herself into a handstand, scissor-kicked around Helpman's neck, and stopped right there.

"*Pas de deux?*" she said, cheeks flushed even under all the smudged makeup.

Helpman's eyes bulged again, this time because his head was pinioned between Mocha's glorious calf muscles. I could see he was stuck and she wasn't about to let him free.

"Mocha," I warned, "watch out for the anvil he has in his mitt."

"Ta."

With no trouble the woman kneed the metal out of Helpman's grip, and then she somehow twisted her torso upward, still in the handstand, to get closer to her captive. That flexibility alone alarmed me — I had no hope of ever touching toes.

"Ivan," she murmured softly, fluttering her enormous false eyelashes, "now I know your real name, let me tell the rest of the story, the part you missed out on."

"You know nothing!" the fake theatre director fumed.

"Wrong. I know everything. *I'm* your harpy."

Some of the steam in the man vanished then. "What?"

"It was me. I wrote the scathing crit. I was the hack that destroyed your father."

"Preposterous!"

"Yet true all the same."

"What nonsense is this? That would make you somewhere in the vicinity of sixty years of age! It was your mother!"

Mocha laughed from her partially upside-down position.

"Oh, I've lived for a *very* long time. One reason my ballet is so good. Lots of practice. What you fail to understand is that I've been doing this mother-daughter routine for centuries. Makes people less suspicious. By the way, I hate to be the bearer of further bad tidings — but your father's film really was awful."

A second later, the woman spun abruptly, having pushed off the floor with her hands, and I heard a loud crack.

Helpman, or Boleslawsky, or whoever the hell he was, fell down across Bruno the Magnificent. His neck was bent at an obscene angle, and spread-eagled together on the stage like that the two men resembled a religious icon thrown together for some exasperating stage-play.

"Jeez. The horror of the world is right here, pal," I muttered as I let go of the drapes and sagged.

Of course Mocha caught me.

This woman, I realized, was capable of anything.

"Roy — are you all right?" she asked quickly. "I heard everything. So sorry I hid. I needed time to figure out things."

"Guessed as much. I make for a good time-waster. And in the end there you more than made up for any earlier faux pas."

"I did?"

"Did you ever."

Leaning back against her shoulder, I could feel the woman's warm breath on my neck.

"I have a question, though — what'd you use on the bastard? Some sort of mixed martial arts?"

"A secret."

She eased us both down to the floor, where I sat on my backside, positioned between two sensational legs in white tights that I'd just seen kill a man.

"Stockholm really was named after you," I realized.

Mocha snuggled her face into my shoulder and granted a couple of kisses. "It was. Seven hundred years ago."

"Huh. You may be an old lady — yet you still manage to save the world and have a town to call your own."

"You OK?"

"I'll live."

I leaned over then, still dizzy, but grabbed the keys from a dead man's pocket and gingerly stood up all by my lonesome.

Be nice to end things there, I guess — with the intimation that Mocha and I lived happily ever after, or at least had a while of it together before I got old and she found a replacement spring chicken to help pass the days of that longevity she reveled in.

Sadly real life rarely lives up to the possibilities.

Less a year later she vanished on me, off on some world tour that never ended, and while I wound up university with a degree that'd also mean nothing in the bona-fide world, I lost it for a few months on end.

Had some mates from uni to do that with.

Remember one such aside: Heidi's head stuck in the bucket like always, and then she arched back and unleashed a long, drawn-out puff of smoke from her lungs.

"Fuck!" she muttered before bursting into a coughing fit.

When it was over she wiped her eyes and smiled a crooked smile.

"Not bad shit", she remarked.

"Gimme the bucket," I suggested impatiently — Heidi might've been my current lay but I was still getting over Mocha, manners be damned — and she looked at me with a vacant expression. "Please," I added just for the sarcastic hell of it.

Voilà. A blue bucket; was sure the other day it was green. I pulled this over between my legs and grabbed the lighter. An old Patra bottle bobbed up and down in water that had a surface of used buds; I stacked it and lit and plunged the thing, and then slowly drew the bottle out of the water, unscrewed its lid and inhaled contents.

She was right. Rough as guts, but within minutes I felt like I was tripping.

Everyone else in the loungeroom was engaged in over-animated conversation, above the sound of Jeff Mills's techno on the stereo, laughing and even singing among themselves. I watched but barely participated. Felt somehow detached. Sat back to listen, barely said boo-hoo even while Heidi fell asleep on my lap.

Another, this time an email she sent me while apparently coming down and declining to use a spell-check or caps.

"...wow that sounds great i couldn't have gone out last night though i went out thursday night to groovetherapy which was quite disappointing grooverider was so sad in stead of saying oh i didn't like those three tracks it was more like picking out the ones that i did like. the thing was sold out and by the end of his 3 hour set half of the crowd was gone, you could see that something was bothering him don't know what, he had a bit of trouble with the decks aswell. but anyway we tried to get into belfast in the morning but the security was so fucked not only would they not let us in they were absolute arseholes about it, it was 6 in the morning and it was closing at 7 or so too, richie sucks eggs. so i hung out with graybaby my main squeeze on saturday got fucked up and i just love la la land i'm still there. it's funny how you have a weekend free from it then next weekend you just happen to do twice as much! like you make up for what you missed out on last weekend! that's what seems to happen to me! it was awesome i loved it so spaced out from some rave the night before and they had these lights that made the velvet curtains look like blood covered, it was ace. i think she was smoking opium! just coz shes asian! whatever, are you going to the free party next sunday at the alexander gardens billy's doing it, it's taken him ages to get it organised it sound like good fun hopefully there will be good weather, did you go to the green ant free party there last year? i had so much fun of my head talking talking talking friends everywhere yay! best be off must send e-mail to marty and teesh in europe bye bye party party party ! love ya heidi."

Two months later, while her friends were off heads on ecstasy at some warehouse rave party, Heidi got herself kidnapped. I wasn't there at the time — had been working the yawn-inspiring paperwork on a case for Arthur, following up an arsonist — but her mates managed to track me down. Gushed about her being snatched by a pink limousine with opaque windows, which I put down to chemicals.

Wasn't sure if I loved the silly cow or cared at all, but said I'd do my best. Which meant doing a fit of old-fashioned sleuthing over a period of twenty-four hours.

Just before midnight on the second day after she vanished I was in an annoyingly floodlit and humid underpass that burrowed deep beneath City Centre.

In the plus column, there was zero traffic at this time, so I could proceed down the middle of the road with carefree abandon, at least till catching sight of a security post.

Had no idea of my plan of action once I reached the Senator's abode — if I reached the place, given the excess of sentries and surveillance doohickeys I expected to encounter between here and there.

The tunnel, only four lanes wide, stretched on and time was precious. I could probably find a more convenient entrance from above, but this route offered a discreet alternative. Working off an excess kilo would never hurt, since I'd been letting myself go.

Having rounded a gradual turn, I spotted my first guard-house directly ahead. Fled the road to press up against a wall, and straight after recoiled — chocolate-brown seepage, hopefully from the Yarra, oozed down the concrete.

In an attempt to steady ransacked nerves, I scrutinized the small, two- or three-man building. How many people were there? What was my excuse for passing through? Hi, saw your lights on, thought I'd drop in? Why should the bozos begin to believe such a rort?

Turns out, however, that fabrications weren't required.

The lights were off, and I couldn't see anybody from this distance. As I carefully stepped over toward the bungalow, I made out no life at all. While this hung as odd, I couldn't deny confirmation when I leaned against the cracked plasti-glass, looked inside, and saw dark shadows in which nothing moved.

The crack puzzled me. This stuff was supposed to be harder than steel, so what could have caused that? And why wasn't it replaced? Poor-man's maintenance didn't ring credible here.

From the wide open door, coming out of hidden speakers in low volume, I caught the sounds of an old big band number about a girl from Kalamazoo. Artie would probably know the name of the tune, but he wasn't here to quiz. There was a camera suspended above the doorway that refused to swivel when I waved up at it. Surely I was target enough for even a malfunctioning device.

I edged forward to the entrance, still puzzling over why there weren't any guards. It might've been a lower-rung concern, but anyway this underpass would slip into the high-security umbrella, being in such close proximity to politicos like Kenbright. Was inconceivable that they'd leave a post unguarded for just a few seconds.

I glanced around, jumpy re: the lack of personnel, riding notions that it had to be a trap. Without taking the time to procrastinate further, I stepped into the building — and tumbled back out again. Stopped myself from landing on my bum by hanging onto the doorframe.

"Shit," I muttered, same time as I dragged eyes from the vivid tableau on the floor of this security booth.

Had glimpsed enough — two methodically gagged and bound guards, throats cut ear-to-ear as apparent afterthought. Dead as discarded doornails. This had to've happened recently. The gashes looked too fresh and blood wept, easing round the edges of vinyl gaffer tape.

I looked unsuccessfully outside in the tunnel proper for some sign of the pricks who'd done this butcher's bit — and straight after plucked up enough wayward courage to go through the guards' pockets. Their holsters may've been empty, but one of the guys had a small pistol tucked up under the left armpit. Bingo. Flimsy as it was, this would do fine.

I extended the gun, a nine millimetre Glock 26, before me as I left the death-trap, turned full circle, and decided upon the bizarre: nobody was here. Who would do this much carnage, only to scarper? Why weren't alarm bells a-klanging? Didn't make for good sense.

My thoughts turned back to Kenbright, and then Heidi.

Whatever the case, if she were with him, I had no time to lose.

I started to jog along the remainder of the tunnel, panting the further I went. Was nowhere near the best condition for this kind of exercise, and I'd forgotten my shorts. Though keeping an eye on the terrain ahead, there was no peep from a single soul. Within minutes I entered a cavernous underground parking garage where priceless vehicles sparkled in uniform rows.

Bent over, I had hands on knees, heart pounding, gasping for air. God, I felt like I was going to die. Finally, I dragged in sufficient oxygen to raise my head.

The Senator's limo was parked over by the elevator shaft.

Even amidst all the other expensive crates it was impossible to miss this car's hot-pink exterior. Kenbright was known for his kinks. Rumour mill said the jerk ironed-out those kinks with a steady succession of young women that people tended to never see again.

The thought of Heidi as a full stop to this chain jolted me.

With the tiny Glock clasped in both hands but arched down a fraction, I weaved from car to car. The limo had its engine off and I couldn't see its driver.

The other titbit I'd gleaned was that this chauffeur had a black belt in karate — meaning she could double-dip as personal bodyguard. The only martial art I'd mastered was making drinks for my boss, so figured the miniature gun would have to fill in for five digits of death.

I reached the limo and peeked through the tinted window.

Oh yeah, our chauffeur was there, all right, but hardly playing coy. All those after-hours karate lessons had been given a single index finger.

Eyes were slitted and stared at some attractive space over my left shoulder. I was tempted to take a gander, though it was pretty obvious she was dead. Couldn't see a mark on her, and there was nothing behind me.

I turned anyway and leaned against the pink vehicle for a while. Had my arms crossed in front of me as I focused on a nearby exit sign. The tummy growled. Damn.

Like to think I was capable enough to mull over the odds and ends and thereby make a decision, but it was pointless trying to slot the pieces into a reasonable whole — none of this clicked, neither disjointed nor lassoed together. The only thing making an impression, the thing that had brought me this far, was Heidi's life being in danger. Mine hanging on the line, too, was beside the point.

Since today's bill of fare appeared to be the act of stealing things from dead bodies, I took the driver's I.D., headed over to the elevators, and then pushed the button. Nothing happened for several seconds. I wondered if the lifts had been locked-down, but I heard a comical 'ding' and a pair of doors slid open.

Having stepped inside I found it too bright in there and was squinting.

"Level Forty-two," I mumbled, swiping the appropriated I.D. card across the panel.

After the doors closed I felt a soft upward motion. Toward — what? An awaiting Senator Kenbright surrounded by bodyguards? A squad of trigger-happy cops? Christ knew, and Christ bloody well cared. For my part, I had no idea and decided to give up on the imagination bit.

Could only try to helping out Heidi.

She deserved that much — I owed her. She'd given me the time of day when most people look at the loser as nothing more than light relief. So I raised the handgun before me, level with my gaze, and waited for the elevator to open.

We stopped at forty-two according to the red-light display, and metal doors slid apart on cue — to an empty, ill-lit hallway. I hopped out and aimed in both directions along the corridor, playing pistolero, but again there were no moving targets. All I saw were a couple of other doors, an antique chest with some purple flowers on top, and a large Renaissance-style painting showcasing a chubby, naked lady on a settee, enjoying a bunch of grapes.

The painting looked the real deal. Old, faded, apparently oil on canvas, though it could've been acrylic or recycled poop for all I knew. Something small caught my eye. When I leaned closer to the picture, I saw a black, oval sticker with white writing — it read 'if?' — stuck to the woman's buttocks.

Right. That would've devalued the thing a significant percentage.

Pulled myself back to the here and now. One of the wooden doors was slightly ajar, so I headed over to that. The closer I got, the more able to distinguish the sound of some kind of slow piano riff. I carefully pushed the door open to a gloomy, average-sized room. Lack of illumination was a worry, though it was the middle of the night, and I guessed this would help mask my movement. This appeared to be a den, with an orderly secretaire and desk, and a bookcase concealing an entire wall. There was another door, closed, that I slowly eased forward.

The master bedroom, I deduced. Who needed Sherlock?

These quarters were huge, with a canopied four-poster bed in the centre, and next to the bed a candelabrum with dozens of burning candles, all of them a different shade of pink wax.

They threw enough light for me to see a naked female form

lying face-down on the bed, hands tied together with a fuchsia stocking, and large red welts crisscrossing her back. She wasn't moving. I crossed the floor, leaned over, and pushed back chestnut hair that obscured the face.

Heidi.

Had already guessed as much. I recognized her backside and the glorious flow of shoulder muscles, cherished the colour of the hair.

This woman's eyes were shut. They'd never reopen.

From the look of the bruising around the neck I assumed she'd been throttled. Working the gun across my forehead, I felt the pain of its sharp sight cutting into the skin. Believe I was attempting to blot out the other pain, the one inside me. She was dead — in the same boat as my old friend Mitch. The same vessel I'd prob'ly be hitching a ride with in a short while.

What a bloody waste.

Sitting on the bed beside Heidi, memories hammered my head from within as I bludgeoned that same head, with the gun, without. This had to stop. The pistol was too flyweight to induce decent physical damage without pulling the trigger, and I needed it to inflict retribution on the arsehole who'd done this.

So, do what Art always dictated. Look around the scene afresh. At the woman in particular. Having done this, I touched her cheek. Vaguely warm.

And I could still hear that damnable piano concerto.

It was louder here, music I recognized, a cheesy piece used in some recent TV advertising. What'd they been hawking? Cars? A mobile phone carrier, more likely.

Tearing gaze from what I told myself was no more than a corpse, I lurched up, and rounded the corner of two further doorways in a blundering hurry.

The source of the music was a flyweight, elderly man wrapped in a towel, toga-fashion, seated before a grand piano. Above the keys he tinkered with was the brand name 'Truffaut', written in flowing gold leaf.

When he saw me in the doorway to his right, the piano player sat up straight.

"Denslow sent you for me, didn't he?"

I glared at the man, spots in my vision. "Denslow? Denslow who?"

"I know he wants to silence me. I've become a liability."

"Dunno what the hell you're talking about. I came for Heidi."

"Oh." Both his mouth and then the man's eyes widened themselves into ridiculously formed 'O's, as if to emphasize the statement. Then they sagged. "You're far too late. She's dead."

"I know that."

"Yes, how silly of me — of course you do."

"Why?" My voice had taken on a croak that sounded pathetic.

"Why, what?"

"Why murder her?"

"Well, now. I haven't an inkling. I think it was accidental — the other times it was definitely an accident. These things happen."

"Right."

The man scratched at his black, rakish, RAF-style moustache. This was obviously dyed, since the thinning hair on top of his head was close to white. I noticed that in doing the scratch he'd stopped playing the piano, yet the music continued unabated. This bloke was all sham.

"Senator Kenbright," I said.

"Yes, yes, that is my name." The man sighed, like he was irritated with my incompetence. "Well, what are you waiting for? Do your thing."

"What thing?"

"The thing you people are paid for. Putting others out of their misery. Why are you waiting?"

"Beats me. Maybe you got me confused with somebody else? And, to be honest, I just changed my mind — I'm here to arrest you. I'm thinking that way you'll have a whole lot more misery ahead."

I took out my phone and made the call.

It felt right. Shooting this bogus piano player would be far too kind.

Besides, it stood to reason that someone had set up all of this. The bundled guards and gift-wrapped chauffeur weren't mere wallpaper. The senator mentioned someone called Denslow.

Better to do this by the book, win a few Tinkertoy medals in the process, and then cry into my drinks later. God — Heidi.

"So, I'm to be arrested," the senator mused. "Might I at least put on something decent? There are bound to be reporters."

"Nah. I like the look of you just as you are. You're lucky I'm letting you stick with the towel."

"May I smoke?"

He lifted a silver case from the top of the piano, but I knocked it across the room.

"Put a lid on it, wanker. Jeez."

Kenbright looked like I'd hurt his feelings. "I am not afraid. I simply served my country," he complained.

"Sure you did, mate. Choice career move."

"You know, aren't you a little young to be a hitman?"

"Hitman? Shit." I could hear the sirens already. "Is this all OK and tidied up to your liking, boss?"

That was the moment Art stepped from shadows by the window. It was so damned obvious now. The set-up, the dead people downstairs, even the convenient gun. This had been some kind of lousy audition.

"You did good, junior," Art said.

"But?"

"But next time, switch off the safety."

"Anything else?"

"Sure. If I were you, I would've drilled the mother-trucker."

That out of the way, Art finally allowed me opportunity to partner-up on cases and start earning real keep as an apprentice dick.

I guess the ballet fiasco and hauling in an insane, serial-killing politician gave me a chest full of gold doubloons in my employer's currency.

So it was that, still smarting on the disappearing act of someone I cared about more than I'd ever let on, and the murder of a replacement I never appreciated, I was summoned by my boss to dinner.

Being a reasonably chilly evening for March, I threw my trenchcoat over a t-shirt that read 'Rock Bottom' across the chest. Yeah, I'd picked up the thing since it matched the moment. Sue me.

Met Art at a dive of a restaurant called ít quái vật, off Victoria Street. He said 7 p.m. so I showed up at 7:30, knowing the bloke always rolled up late. This time he didn't.

Settled in at a table near cowboy-style swing doors to the kitchen, beneath a glitzy, late-period painting of Elvis Presley, he was wearing a rumpled suit and beige straw hat on the back of his head, shades on Darren McGavin in '70s TV show *Kolchak: The Night Stalker*. Before him were the remains of a bowl of phở. And instead of telling me off he merely paused between mouthfuls to tap his watch.

That worried some.

Having pulled out the diner chair opposite the other man, I sat and placed elbows on the crowded table.

I pulled out a wobbly diner chair opposite, sat, and placed my elbows on a laminated table that still conspired to have stains in the surface.

"You eaten?" Art inquired, rice noodles and meat swirling around his teeth and hampering articulation.

"Sure."

"Drink?"

I examined the older man's empty glass. "What're you having, Boss?"

ART: "Beer."

ME [lighting a cigarette with the classic Zippo lighter that'd once belonged to Mocha and still added salt to the wound]: "Huh. You're getting soft on me?"

ART: "No, but I need a clear head."

ME: "What for?"

While saying this I summoned over a waitress, a cutie giftwrapped in a powder-blue silk áo dài.

ME: "Two more beers. VB."

After this lady scuttled off in her tight-fitting dress I glanced back to the other man, waiting for a tardy reply.

He swallowed, dabbed at his mouth with a grubby paper napkin, and smiled. "Business," he said.

Now I stared. Had to take a quick drag on the ciggie. "Business."

"Roy, I've been figuring things, working the books."

"The devil you have."

ART: "Laugh it up."

ME: "I think I'll need a few more drinks before I find that amusing. Right now it's just plain astonishing."

ART: "No choice. The business is in the red."

ME: "You going to fire me?"

ART: "Whatever gave you that impression?"

I smiled, having leaned back, arms crossed. "Then make me a partner."

"Pfft. Maybe I *will* fire you."

The waitress had returned with two glasses. The heads were too big and they dripped everywhere as I placed one before me and shoved the other across the table.

"Then who'll shine your shoes?" I said.

ART: "Sure I can find better."

ME: "Maybe. Prob'ly." [I clinked my glass against the older

man's] "So what can we do?"

Art leaned back his head, finished the beer in one long swig, and then made a signal to the staff for two more. That settled he pushed his bowl to one side.

"Listen, kid, we need an angle, something that separates us from the divorce gigs and motor-accident fraud rorts. We're up against too much competition."

And they're way more professional. "Go on," I said.

"These things don't cover our costs."

Or Arthur's expensive habits. I tossed the old guy a grin instead — better that some observations went unspoken.

ART: "So I got to thinking: What can we do that's different, yet still has decent moula in it to bankroll the business and thereby keep us afloat?"

ME: "I'm not bending any kneecaps for you, Art. I'm hardly tough enough."

ART: "Yeah, that frailty of yours did cross my mind."

That was when I noticed the butter knife in his mitt.

Something he'd apparently brought with him as this was too classy for these premises and didn't fit the ethnic decor. In the half-light I could see it was silver-plated, with fancy art-deco curvature.

Meanwhile, the waitress returned to our table carrying two more beers, at which point Art very casually twisted around and stabbed the woman in the gut.

As drinks hit the floor and smashed and the waitress crumpled in a heap, I pushed back in my chair, shocked.

"Bejesus, Art — what—?!"

Artie took his time. He raised his brow as he first watched the woman writhing beneath us on the floor, and then used that serviette to wipe blood from his knife – thence to place it in a leather pouch that contained its relatives, a fork and a soup spoon.

Throughout this slow, deliberate process he yabbered on in a voice hard to hear above shrieks and howls.

"Speaking of frailty, as we were, I wrote that very word on a whiteboard, erased the last two letters — and found our niche. Well, actually, *you* did. That Stockholm frail of yours."

I said nothing, but could feel blood drain from my face as I clenched my right fist on the table.

ART: "Relax, boy-o. I haven't taken her on as assignment — but all the same you better be ready to have your heart busted and boiled in this biz."

ME: "What the hell are you talking about? What does this have to do with Mocha?"

ART: "Nothing. Everything."

I didn't know how Art ignored the screams right beside us, pretty much in his lap. This was goddamned awful. Where was the rest of the staff? The cops and paramedics?

"She alerted me, Roy, to the fact that supernatural fruits like her are out there — and these bastards're causing mayhem. Therein lies our angle. Take a leaf out of the *Ghostbusters* textbook to work clean-up chores. We'll be swimming in dosh. How say you, kid? You with me on this?"

My eyes fixed on the woman on the floor behind Arthur, who was writhing and...changing shape. Big tufts of hair sprouting and then receding, talons shredding the linoleum.

"Um... What about her?"

ART [screwing up his nose]: "Bit of an over-theatrical demo. She'll be dead in a few seconds."

ME: "Why?"

ART: "Silverware." [The old man shrugged, and started again on his soup] "In case you hadn't noticed, there's a full moon on the rise out there."

Six years later I'd begun picking up the pieces of my boss-cum-partner.

On this particular October night had already clocked off at the office and didn't need to put up with the shit after hours as well.

Arthur Miller was a mere six inches from my face and here I was choking on words.

Not thanks to some family-history insecurity fix, but because of the invisible fumes that billowed up and over that precious half-foot — lack of clarity doing nothing to temper the beasts of several hours' bourbon.

"For crap's sake, Art, how much of this bloody stuff have you gobbled up?" I asked as I leaned back, adding a reprieve of a further few centimetres.

The ulterior smell in this down/out pub was tolerable at such a fair distance since the local miasma erased it. Scooping up from the table one bottle, I inspected its label: Death Adder Whiskey — Australia's second legal sour-mash whiskey, they claimed on the back. Brewed employing a sour-mash process used in America to produce Tennessee whiskey and Kentucky Bourbon Whiskey, made non-potable from a further stir-fry of Australian corn, rye and barley.

"Sounds like its namesake," I mused, spilling myself a glass from the dregs of flagon #3. I downed two inches with one gulp. Yep — spot on.

Art placed elbows on that filthy, sticky table, between grey cigarette droppings and wet ring-marks aplenty. His face then sagged into supportive hands.

"Nah. Tolerable drop. Reckon it was the line in the dunny that pushed me over the edge," the old man muttered.

Not that he was talking up queues — I knew the kind of lines my senior partner liked to indulge in. Employing a rolled-up plastic ten-buck note with Mary Gilmore looking prude on the outside and 'Banjo' Patterson riding roughshod atop a galloping horse within.

Either way, this was far from fun.

"Why'd you call me down here?" I whined.

"Had better plans?"

"Reckon there were healthier ones."

"Bullshit, Roy."

"Look, some of us do have lives, twee as they might seem."

Art cocked his head. "Mootable."

"Still."

"What, that ballerina you're still pining for?"

This made me break eye contact. "Ballet dancer. And no. She moved on to better curtain-calls a long time ago. You know that."

"So why you still carrying the torch, kid?"

"There's no torch here."

With that, Artie guffawed at something he wasn't keen to share — but then got all conspiratorial on me. "Listen in. You heard tell of the Beer Monster?"

This made me laugh, annoyance aside. "What, some fiendish devil that swings by after you've been on a bender, erasing most memories, stealing all your cash, and sending weird-arse text messages to a good proportion of your mates?"

"There's the one."

"Seem to remember one occasion when he nicked my left shoe." I caught a waitress's eye to order two pints. "Never did find that shoe," I continued as I returned attention to my partner. "Bastard. So, what, you're hot on his heels here?"

"Don't jest, sonny jim." Art's eyes darted first right, and then left. He scooted his chair forward to lean in real close, offering up those heady fumes again. "It's real."

"What's real?"

"The *Beer Monster*."

"Sure, okay. Hangs out with the Sandman, hmm?" I sighed as I shoved further away again and gratefully stuck my nose in the glass the waitress passed to me. "Got a signature tune crooned by

The Chordettes — how do the lyrics go again? 'Mister Beer Monster, bring me a drink, dum-dum-dum,' right?"

"Har-de-har. Laugh it up."

"Better than getting all depressed, Boss."

"*Listen to me*, Roy — I'm not pissing about."

"Well, you're hardly being serious."

"No — I am." Art shook his head, a drunkard's toss, but his faded eyes pushed wild. "Spite," he muttered. "Spite is the method of your ungluing. I've done my homework, looked into the history."

"What, using an empty pair of beer glasses as your spectacles?"

Art handled this flat quip in the manner deserved — ignored it. Instead the man was speedily spouting facts and figures with surprising vigour, even if half the vocab was slurred.

"Listen. In 1685, the Cistercian monastery brewery of St. Trappe in Soligny — that's in France — reported several violent deaths over a three-month period. The only eyewitness swore black-and-blue that he'd spotted *un monstre de bière jaune...* A great yellow monster. You hear me?"

"Too clearly. Try keeping your voice down."

"There's more," Art said.

"Can't you write it down on a memo? You're not paying me this time of night."

"Overtime rates, kid."

"Huh. Trouble is, when I remind you tomorrow you'll play dumb."

"Do you want to hear more?"

"Can I say 'no'?"

"You'll regret that. Let me tell you more and decide."

"Then it'll be too late," I groaned.

"Where was I? The U.K.?" Art barged on, woozily oblivious. "Okay, let's cross channel to England. The London Beer Flood of 1814, when 1.47 million litres of the stuff, I'm talking beer, beer gushed out into Tottenham Court Road, where—"

"Where you were waiting with your glass."

"Hah. Yeah. Keep 'em flying, kiddo. This infamous beer flood actually destroyed two houses, damaged a pub, and killed up to nine people. They're still not sure how many. Straight after, *The Times* newspaper correspondent Arnold Soissons jotted down our first recorded use of the expression 'beer monster' — attributed to a hysterical survivor before the man was locked up in a local funny farm."

"That figures."

Twitching of the left cheek was the only response I got this time round. Ignoring me always was Art's modus operandi.

"Back a bit in 1516, William IV, Duke of Bavaria, passed the *Reinheitsgebot* or purity law — word has it — to deal not only with cleaner ingredients but to subdue some side-effect monstrosities that developed when corrupted ales were brewed: *Ungetüme,* as this law mentions between the lines. 'Course you need to know your German and have a handy magnifying whatsit."

This nonsense made me sigh. "Art... You're losing me. What's this got to do with anything?"

"Apparently 'ungetüme' is Kraut-language for monsters."

"Apparently?"

"Depends where you look online."

I delicately raised eyebrows but declined to comment.

"Charles Dickens'd be pleased, too," my partner rambled on, as if citing famous historical dead people would restore faith, "since during the Industrial Revolution there buzzed numerous reports of people being mashed instead of the mixing of the starch source with hot water. Unexplained deaths, most butcher-jobs."

"So? Wasn't that why Charlie wrote a lot of his books, motivated by the shit that happened back then?"

"All right. All right. So you want recent facts?"

"Wouldn't mind."

"How about an 'accident' that killed seven workers at a brewery in Mexico City in 2013 — covered up by authorities, but not before a dying, partially dismembered cleaner reported the presence of *el monstruo amarillo*... The yellow monster."

I toyed at my third drink, swirling contents to recreate a head. I'd give the old fart this much: He at least attempted to do research, something I was never overly fond of applying.

"People can read anything into mouldy historical documents," I said.

"Kid, don't quote me at me. We both know there's a helluva lot out there we can't explain off. This is our business."

Our office motto... Investigators of the occult and paranormal. Meaning my ex-girlfriend was immortal and last week we'd exorcised one of Satan's little helpers.

What? It made a buck or two.

"If you look deeper," Art waffled on, "and can decipher old Persian, you'll find chatter of a brewery *dīv* in the Ebla tablets from about 2,500 BC, while eight hundred years later the Babylonian Code of Hammurabi had a provision addressing preternatural activity in fermented cereal grain beverages. So you see?"

"No. See what?"

"See that this bastard's been there all along, hiding out more than four millennia."

"Mm-hmm." Far more patient than I was.

"Trust me on this. Who's the experienced one here? Who's been dealing with all the freaks, nuts, queers and grotesques since before you entered high school? Who damned well taught you every single thing you know?"

That was when the soliloquy shorted-out, thank God.

"Dunno," I said. "Who?"

"You're looking at him."

"Debatable, if we're talking up your own fine self," I

muttered. "Ninety percent of my on-the-job training you were passed out somewhere, and the other ten percent I either tucked you in or covered up." A smile toyed with the right-hand corner of my mouth. "The Beer Monster got his claws in way before I was born."

"Still."

"Still, what?"

"Tonight, I'm going to catch the prick!"

"That so?"

"That indeed so."

"How? By exhaling on him? And anyway, shouldn't you be drinking beer instead of bourbon?"

"Beer either side of the rotgut is fine."

Rolling my eyes wasn't exactly a voluntary reflex by that point. "Okay, so this thing *does* exist. What're you going to do? — Whisk the bugger off to an AA meeting, where there're no longer any true believers and he vanishes in a puff of smoke or better yet melts into an inconsequential puddle of ale?"

"No need. I have this."

Art conjured up a chrome hip flask with a hexagram engraved on the side closest to me. He unscrewed its lid and offered the thing my way. I cautiously took a whiff, expecting either Polmos Spirytus 160-proof Rectified Spirit or pee, but found neither. This smell reminded me of summer holidays at my gran's place, when she sat in the kitchen all day pickling onions.

"Vinegar?" I checked.

"White vinegar. If a little of it is guaranteed to remove beer stains from garments, a half-litre should be enough to polish off this monster."

I breathed out loud. "So. What colour is he?"

"Who?"

"This critter of yours. Blond? Tan? Half-and-half?"

Art stared through me, eyes attempting to focus and a sweaty, glossy sheen to the skin on his face. "I haven't the faintest idea."

I was sure he didn't.

There would be no marauding supernatural creature here — nothing to gun down using silver bullets, peg with a wooden stake, or bamboozle via the New Testament.

But Art rang right; a personal demon was at play. His very own Beer Monster had slowly eaten at him from the inside, destroying family, dismembering career, and eventually trashing one very unfortunate liver.

The disoriented geriatric I observed slowly passing on in this bar over the course of half an hour was forty-four years of age. He looked sixty-four, a yellowing tinge to his skin and eyeballs, his forehead slick. That aroma I mentioned hung worse than ever, and it wasn't just his breath but the very pores of the skin that reeked.

Art suddenly winced, clutched at his side, and fell off the chair.

For a moment I suspected he was indulging in a spot of theatre sports — the man could be a surprisingly funny bugger — but when he didn't get up, I fretted some and helped him back to his seat, suggesting I call an ambulance.

"Nah, nah, no need, kid. Just need to take a leak. I feel like a dyke that's about to be breached."

Twenty minutes later as I polished off my fourth pint of beer, I mulled over the fact my partner still hadn't returned, so stooped to a house call.

When I entered the toilet, the overhead fluorescent light was on the blink, flicking on and off as it swung wildly, but by the strobe-effect illumination I saw enough.

Something ten feet tall. Big, amber-coloured, slick, bubbly, and bulbous-veined — holding aloft my boss as it smashed his head into a long mirror above the sinks — over and over. There was broken glass and buckets of blood all over the filthy linoleum floor before I could begin to nut out an appropriate response that didn't border on panic.

Thing was... What the fuck stunted a Beer Monster, aside from white vinegar?

I didn't have a gun—never got a license, was somehow against them in spite of the mad risks in our dodgy profession.

But Art's Smith & Wesson lay on the floor right nearby. I saw it in one of the flashes of light. So I swooped quick as possible, clear of that monster doing calisthenics with Art's skull, and then I fired without aiming, emptying it in seconds.

Kept pulling the trigger on an empty chamber for much longer afterward, until I realized: The vinegar wasn't required. So much for research.

This was never going to be a police job.

After recovering a modicum of sense to wash my face clear of tears, blood and off-yellow globules, I fetched the owner of the bar. I don't know what he was doing while I was screaming and shot his bathroom to pieces. Once I showed him the tableau in there, this guy declined to invite any form of authority. Even so, I had a call of my own to make.

By the time Art's seventeen-year-old daughter Suzie made it over she'd inherited her father's side of the business, while I'd leap-frogged in the firm and gained a junior partner.

When mandatory crocodile tears were done — I knew the girl didn't care one iota for her old man — we did a labourious spot of tidying up and arranged things for my late partner's corpse. Then I escorted Suzie from that stinky pub and we walked through an empty carpark outside.

"Jeez. That was...enlightening," said Suzie, surprisingly chipper.

"I know. Nature of the biz."

"So what happens now?" the girl mumbled while looking straight ahead at God knows what in the darkness.

I glanced at this bookish blonde-with-pigtails beside me. "Why not sell me your half? You're a kid. Don't want to get involved in all the voodoo rubbish we have to contend with. It's dangerous and the returns barely cover cost. I'll give you a fair price."

"No way." Suzie stopped, looked at me with an oddball kind of resolve, and pushed back her glasses. "Dad wouldn't've wanted me to sell out."

"How the hell can you know what Artie would or wouldn't have wanted? You barely knew the bastard — and fair enough too."

"Still."

"Still?" I felt marginally ill. "Go on. Spill it."

"Well, this's the family business."

"You're kidding?"

"No. No, Roy, I'm not. It meant something to him, and he *was* my father. There has to be a Miller involved. What's brawn without brains?"

"Shit." I shook my head, deducing I was in way over that underused body part. "Great. So what happens now?"

"Now?" Suzie suddenly clapped hands together and assumed a zany smile on her mush that scared me. "Now we get new business cards made."

"Hold it, just a sec—"

"Of course, there's someone I know who knows someone else — and I always had a hankering for baby blue. Don't you? I can see them now, in satin-finish: 'Scherer and Miller, Investigators of the Paranormal and Supermundane'. *Sweet.* Happy Hallowe'en, partner!"

3: MORE RECENTLY

I stepped up to the plate to swat King Tut from behind.

Sure it was cowardly, but also a pretty nifty manoeuvre, done without a moment to second-guess myself or opportunity to nut out a different course of action.

His skull was relatively unprotected, an obvious target tarted-up in tattered, 4000-year-old bandages. A neck thicker than my waist propped up that head — quite some feat given the extra girth I'd put on in recent months of alcoholic mayhem and loafing about on the couch.

The blow wasn't intended to kill him. No need to get blood on my hands, though any drops he did have probably evaporated a couple of millennia before.

Trouble was that the mummy apparently sensed me behind him, and second-guessed my intentions to boot. He ducked as I swung the gun, and I ended up glancing the handle off ancient gift-wrapping instead of getting in a heavy enough whack to knock this pharaoh senseless.

Then, while I was off balance, he turned and grabbed me by the throat, huge fingers digging deep into my larynx, and a second later I'd been deprived of both the capacity to squeal and an ability to breathe. Long-dead guy lifted me up one handed; my shoes no longer touched the ground, and I was ogling this human Band-Aid inches from my face, a dribble of saliva in the corner of a snarling mouth that had no teeth.

With his free hand he slapped me once, twice, a third time.

Left me seeing stars, and other delusionary paraphernalia. Felt like this time, finally, the gig might truly be up. Thoughts shunted in between the sparkling stars, images of Mocha and Heidi and even Suzie, and what would likely happen to her if I gave up the ghost, pulling up personal tent-pegs here and now.

I still had the gun in my right fist. Could pop him in the jaw, put a slug in his parchmenty eye, hopefully get this over with, but something held me back. I wouldn't call this a conscience — it was more like stubborn, idiotic madness.

Another slap knocked me silly. I could see specks of blood on the man's chunky, off-white covered face. Not his blood.

Mine.

So I swung at my own blood, right at a big splash of it on his forehead, lined up like a bull's-eye. The gun barrel bounced off, but the man shook his head, like it hurt. I tried again, and again. The fourth time rocked it — I fell flat on my bum, oxygen restarted, while the mummy stormed about like he was doing some kind of blind Indian rain dance, clutching his skull, screaming.

Then he barnstormed the wall, head first, and knocked himself out. Lay at my feet, unmoving. At least he'd cut the over-dramatics.

My head was swimming enough as was. I had to road test my voice, to see if it still worked. "Sleep tight," I muttered. Nothing more cutting came. The weak quip'd have to do — even if I did have an audience.

Suzie was bound and gagged and half her body bandaged up over in a corner, next to a widescreen TV, like she'd been placed there as a second-thought decoration. Guess King Tut had been working on mummification for some Christmas season cheer. I went straight over, leaned down, and touched her cheek. Her eyes were wide, even the one on the left that was swollen and ringed with blue-black.

Without waiting for applause, I undid her wrists and pulled off the material jammed into her mouth. Suze could deal with the feet herself.

After breathing deeply a few times, apparently relishing the opportunity, my girl looked straight at me.

"You look awful. D'you always have to make it so hard for yourself, Roy? You could've just shot him, or used the ceremonial dagger of Antioch. You had ample opportunity. Pfft."

I glowered at her. "D'you want me to put the gag back on?"

Couple of months back I started dating a stunner named Lilith and this bordered more upon infatuation than anything I had experienced in years.

To be completely honest I'd avoided women — aside from Suzie, who didn't count — since Heidi. Threw myself into work, classic films, and alcohol, though the order of these three things tended to alternate in favour of the latter. The only real spirits I caroused with came from a bottle.

What Lilith saw in me, I had no idea, but when I peered at her my eyes hurt. Really. Woman was so seriously drop-dead gorgeous that it impeded my vision.

Even better she never asked me about what it was I did for a living, and I never thought to ask her in return. Ninety percent of our relationship we spent between bedcovers anyway.

Funny thing was that the more time we had together, the less well I felt in general — and I'm not talking up just the eyes. I'd taken to skipping out on work and wasted time away from Lilith dosing myself up on cold and flu medication or lying in a heap on the couch.

Suzie started dropping in like meals on wheels, delivering pots of chicken soup and orange juice by the gallon.

I should've seen the signs — we'd been in the biz long enough.

But I always was a slow learner. For crap's sake, don't tell Suzie.

The first thing Lilith did was powder her nose.

Unzipped a tobacco-coloured Louis Vuitton purse in the same manner a lioness, basking in the sun on an African savannah, tends to flick its tail—in a deceptive, lazy kind of way, but in reality quick and precise.

She dropped her hand in the bag and fiddled about a few moments before long, slender fingers emerged with a compact. Leaning toward the half-length mirror attached to the wardrobe, as I said, she powdered her nose.

I'd never seen anybody do it with such style.

Straight after eyes in the mirror shifted to mine, she smiled a fraction, and then changed her mind to blow a kiss.

I'm pretty certain it missed, and that was the point. Attention returned to the looking glass, she adjusted the bra strap on her left shoulder, straightened out a dress strap next to that, rotated both shoulders to make the ensemble sit better, and pushed hair back.

"What're you looking at, babe?" Lilith said, distracted.

I didn't answer. Just stared at the beauty in that reflection and found it remarkable that a serpent could sit so pretty.

"Snake got your tongue?" She seemed to know my every thought, and that was spooky. Not that it mattered now, I guess. Her laughter was husky as it drifted around me. I loved that sound. I loved her. Thought the feeling was mutual, but I'd begun to suspect I was dead wrong.

On top of me now, the aroma of lilacs intense, she pressed her face close as possible to mine, so that our eyes met and her two hazel peepers became one in my struggling vision.

"Cyclops," she whispered — a recent game of affection, yet right now her tone sounded more vicious than vivacious.

Straight off the bat she broke away, sat up, and stared. "Well, you are rather boring today, my love. You could put in a little more effort."

After easing herself off my lap, the woman headed into the

kitchenette, and pushed two slices of bread into the pop-up. The cap was off the tequila and she was swigging out of the bottle. Wandering that savannah again, eyes pushing wild, before a return to civilization and pouring a shot into a glass.

She paced the kitchen waiting for toast. The way she walked took her out of my sight every now and then, but I could hear her breathing and still smelled the perfume.

"You got any Vegemite?" she asked. "Oh wait, found it!" Her next pace took her to the fridge, where she peered inside. "Oh crap. Margarine? I hate margarine, you know that. Why couldn't you get Western Star butter instead? A girl might get the feeling that you don't care about what she wants." The toast popped, and then she was laughing to herself as she spread condiments. In her next breath singing Foghorn Leghorn.

"Oh, doggy, you're gonna get your lumps. Oh, doggy, you're gonna get some bumps..."

The way she stood there on the linoleum floor, I was watching from behind. She definitely knew how to move that body in that tight satin dress — truth is she always did, especially in my field of vision. Her hips swayed as she spread and serenaded, and it was a mesmerizing sight.

Finally, breakfast was over, followed by a sizable slug of tequila, and she came back into the bedsit — with the bottle — to stand before me.

"I'd offer you some brekky," she murmured, "but I have a feeling you'd just play mum. You know?" After she swirled the tequila around a bit, the woman glanced at it and back to me. "So, what's your poison? ... Oh, wait, you've already had it." She leaned over me on the couch and pried away the empty tumbler that'd been stuck in my mitt for the past half hour. "How's that paralysis coming along, babe?"

She put a playful finger to my mouth, though I couldn't feel it. Also wasn't able to catch the lilac anymore.

"No need to answer. Shouldn't be long now. Probably your

vision will start botching next."

I could still see her clear enough, but the edges of my eyesight were starting to get haggard, and that haggardness crept in from all sides. She sniffed the glass that she took from me and frowned.

"Say, you can smell the extra bonus stuff a mile off. You really have only yourself to blame. Someone who was a bit more cautious would've whiffed this before the first sip. But you just love your booze, don't you? Down the hatch before you even stop to breathe." She sighed. "Well, I was nice, anyway — at least this concoction isn't as painful as others. It's also not very quick. Sorry about that."

She was right. At that moment I felt nothing, senses numb, but as I say it'd been over thirty minutes according to the big, kitsch, 3D crucifixion-scene clock on the wall.

There was a query nagging away at the back of my noggin. I just wished I could enunciate it through dead lips, or express it to her with fading eyes; some kind of mental Morse code. Hell, sign language would be fine, if my fingers still worked.

The question was a simple, one-word no-brainer: Why?

She picked up the phone and made a call. "That's right," I heard her say, "he's not going anywhere. Problem solved. Uh-huh. A few minutes more."

Right about then the lights for me went out.

A slap brought me back to consciousness.

Made out a small white saucer held up a few inches from my face, with a small lump of distorted yellow gunk sitting on it.

She was showcasing the thing like a '50s Tupperware party hostess.

"It's incredible," she says, "what these days a girl will do for a tawdry soul. I'm running low, Roy. You'll be my refill. I do have to say thank you."

That was when she lost balance on her pumps, just as the tawdry dress front shifted and something created a pointy bulge there beneath the material.

"I do believe you've pilfered enough sustenance, lady."

The voice making this declaration was said in such a sweet, singsong tone that I barely recognized it. It came from just behind my assailant, who turned a fraction, and shuddered. Lilith nodded her head in a bouncy kind of way, the face sagged like a sack of old potatoes, and she slid down to the lino.

Looked like gravity did get the better of stiff upper lip on this occasion.

Suzie was standing in her place, shorter in height but immeasurably superior eye-candy right now. Had our blessed silver shiv in her right hand, a long hunting number, and the knife had just been used to skewer the other woman and her sexy wardrobe — thank God I wasn't the only one up for poking the carte du jour.

Suzie kicked the corpse once, and then arched an eyebrow at me. "I'd say she's gone to join her succubae sister demon queens Mahalath, Agrat Bat Mahlat, and Naamah. Wouldn't you?"

Had something tinkering with my vision — I'll swear it was sweat — and couldn't clear this away since my arms were still paralyzed.

Having poured a cup of something foul down my throat, Suzie stepped back. I could feel life returning to deadened limbs, and rediscovered anew the power to speak

"Jesus wept, Suze. Timing."

"Not bad, right?"

"I'd give you a round of applause but my hands are otherwise occupied."

"Then I'll try to picture it." She gave me the once-over and laughed. "Say, don't you have any sense of shame? Where on earth are your clothes?"

Only thing I could think up on the fly?

Grabbing the beastie by the tail, since he didn't have a flea-collar and I had no intention of venturing anywhere near a foamy set of canines. 'Sides, Rex had this huge empennage that was like shaggy rope. Felt like I was back in high school doing a losing bout of tug-of-war — before I got gunned-down and laid-up in hospital, I mean.

"Careful!" hollered Suzie from her place several feet up a ghost gum, all verbal help when I needed this least. "They say lycanthropy is a form of rabies — don't let the brute bite!"

Me? I figured sticking round this huge monster's nether-regions meant he couldn't easily snap jaws on a stray bodypart, though he tried like hell — by pummeling me into trunks and branches at head height in the parkland around us.

Also, shouting at the top of lungs seemed like a good way to keep me from screaming with fear as much as pain. "Thought—" *Ouch!* "—that we didn't—" *Ow!* "—have rabies in—" *Urgh!* "—Australia?"

I mean you'd yelp a lot if you hung onto the tail-end of a werewolf that stood three metres tall when he wasn't stooping to try a chomp.

"Japan and Singapore too," Suze soapboxed above insane growls, a flopping tongue, breaking flora. "And classical rabies has been eradicated in the UK, but bats infected with a related virus have been found in the countryside."

"This isn't a bloody bat!"

"I realize that."

"And I don't give a rat's arse about the mother country!"

"Not my point."

"Then get back down here! Earn your pay!"

"Fat chance! This gig's unpaid, Roy — and it's my birthday. I'm coming nowhere near that thing."

"Thought you were scared of heights?" I threw this comment back in between collisions and much thrashing.

The girl was quick on reply: "Depends on circumstances."

Yeah, circumstances were a moot point.

Two minutes before the fun, games, and rolling in hay with a therianthropic hybrid wolf-like creature (Suzie's description, I swear), we'd been nowhere near a case — my partner and I were out for an evening stroll.

Not exactly hand-in-hand, but this wasn't work-related.

We'd shared ales at the Slaughtered Lamb, celebrating the girl's twentieth birthday — meaning we'd been joined at the hip going on for two-and-a-half years. Thirty-odd months of chasing down spooks, ghouls and assorted vermin.

It figured that the kid would be born on October 31. Hallowe'en and all that.

"You should be out partying with mates," I'd uttered into my glass at one fair stage. "Not sharing beverages with an ancient fart like me."

"Hardly old. Only ten years' diff between us."

"Old enough."

Suzie had placed her current drink carefully onto the table. "Don't have any. Friends, I mean." She'd then pushed loose blonde hair behind the left ear. "Not surprising, given the hours we keep."

"And the job we plumb."

"Not to mention the types we attract."

"Right?"

Don't know what possessed me — maybe it was the hangdog look on Suzie's kisser. Certainly her subdued demeanour helped. I'd placed my fingers over her left hand.

"No fuss. You'll always have me, ol' mum," I announced.

That made the girl smile, and I've got to admit it'd made me chirpy. Did I tell you Suzie has this tiny mole on the lower right side of her chin, a charming one barely visible from a distance? Up close, just then, I found it vaguely attractive.

So I'd paid our tab and taken her to the adjacent park with an oddball ulterior motive in mind. Breezed past some kid in a sheet, shades of Casper, and a teenager done up like Lon Chaney, Jr. as the Wolf Man.

As we walked through the trees in the dark I even removed my Stetson as a sign of semi-inebriated respect. Let her carry my gun, which is about as romantic as I got — she tucked the Smith & Wesson Model 10 into her rouge handbag and smiled deeper still.

Yes, the alcohol had softened the whine in Suzie's tone. She looked a million bucks in that short red one-piece and heels — had apparently grown up while I was busy staking bogeymen. When she took off spectacles and peered up at me on tiptoe, all blue eyes, I was set to sweep the annoyance into my arms.

Which was when she sneezed.

And sniffled. A lot. Shattering the illusion.

"What's up?" I'd asked as she put glasses back on and blew her nose into a floral hankie that clashed with the dress.

"Allergies."

"Huh."

I propped the hat on the back of my head, lit a cigarette — and froze.

A memory had come home to roost from yesterday's paper. People slain, actually ripped apart, just a block from this piece of real estate. A speedy glance at the pitch-black sky had confirmed a full moon. I even had a flashback of Art's Vietnamese waitress. Chiefly, however, the clue came in the sound of something big that lurked noisily nearby in poorly lit underbrush.

One thing to double-check. "You're allergic to dogs, right?"

"Yep — why?" Suzie had nodded, blinking in the direction of the ruckus.

"Scoot up this tree, kid."

"Huh?"

"No questions. Listen to Uncle Roy. Up the gum." I turned Suzie about and gave her a leg-up in the direction of overhead branches, and she'd climbed with surprising dexterity till out of sight. Could still hear the sniffing, however.

"Cut the waterworks, will you?"

"Immunoglobulin E responses aren't exactly voluntary," the kid griped from her perch, even as she settled in. "And what on earth *is* that noise?"

"I'd say it's the source of your allergen getting set to tuck into light snacks. Us."

"What kind of dog is that big?"

"Doubt this's a dog. Close relative, though."

When Rex had charged and I reached for my revolver, I found sweet nothing in the holster. The fag tumbled from my mouth, I'd grabbed for the tail, et voilà.

Back-story told.

Next thing I was winded and likely had a rib busted — so much for wasted time reminiscing. Rex'd pulled a meat-in-the-sandwich swifty when he threw himself backwards into a solid elm, me in between. As I fell forward to the ground I realized I'd stupidly let go of his tail. Inches from my face was a snarling snout that showcased atavistic traits even while sharing a hot breath. Meantime a pair of yellow eyes inspected my everything like I was an ethnic restaurant picture menu.

No doubt about it — I was all set to become another kind of meaty victual.

"There's a good boy," I mumbled, lifting a twig and waving it about. Yes, I was desperate. Yes, the gesture ached. "Good, good doggie. You wanna fetch...?"

That was when Rex surprised me.

He sat back on his haunches, panting, the drool spilling from a corner of his mouth, and he waited. Even seated the bugger was taller than me.

So I swallowed hard and tossed the flimsy piece of timber. This manoeuvre also hurt like buggery and I couldn't lob far, but pooch set off and returned with it coated in slobber that made me fret — didn't werewolves pass on their mojo via saliva?

I needed a replacement toy, post haste.

"I have the gun, remember?" This was Suzie in a remarkably steady tone from overhead branches, p'raps intelligent enough not to spook our four-footed friend. "But it isn't loaded with silver bullets."

"Not sure we can afford them these days anyway," I muttered.

That's when I recalled an old yarn I loved as a kid — written by Henry Lawson, this story was called 'The Loaded Dog'.

Concerned three gold miners in outback Australia, their dog, and a stick of dynamite.

Knew there was a reason I kept a similar stick tucked away in the inside breast pocket of my suit jacket. More than once had considered setting this off under Suzie's bum, but it'd still collected lint for months.

I took the thing out, found my half-smoked cigarette still smouldering on the turf at my feet, lit the fuse, and threw this glowing TNT into dark trees.

"Sick it, Rex!"

Hounddog leapt away, seemingly too fast — with no luck he'd be straight back and we'd both be blown to kingdom come. But seconds passed as he bustled about the brush in the dark, rummaging for the missing stick.

Finally, an explosion shook the ground and felled nearby shrubberies. Bits and pieces of wood, dirt and dead dog rained down.

"Yuck!" Suzie groaned. "I have chunks on me!"

At least she'd cut the sniveling and I laughed in spite of diabolical pain from my chest. "Enough to make a coat?"

Jack London'd be maybe proud.

"I want you to purge the thing and take it away."

"Nothing like a spot of purging," I agreed.

We were standing on the threshold of a sunroom, into which late-afternoon rays drifted through gently swaying curtains. The bantam-sized man beside me, the one who'd suggested the purge, was dressed in a smart suit that whiffed of mildew, mothballs and a bottom-line fragrance of urine. He looked like the Hollywood actor David Niven right before he died: classy, British, a moustache, ancient. Over the other side of the space, on a solid oak desk, was a vintage Underwood 11 — 1940s and equally creaky.

"So what was it you wanted purged?"

"That typewriter. All the keys and the spacebar work, except the 'H'," the old guy said with some pride, his voice dusty. "They're the original glass-top tombstone keys."

"Neat," I said. I blew out my cheeks and made a loud sigh, didn't care if it were rude. "Honestly, though, looks like you gandered in the wrong parts of the Yellow Pages. We're not removalists or pawnbrokers."

"Didn't think you were, Mister—?"

"Scherer. Roy Scherer. We deal with stuff that's, well — crap." I was struggling to place my finger on precisely what it was we do, and 'crap' was a good word for it. Then I realized I had a better escape hatch. "Suzie, why don't you tell the gent?"

This was the perfect cue for my hyperactive 'assistant' to jump into the fray.

"Scherer and Miller, Investigators of the Paranormal and Supermundane," she announced, as our baby-blue business card spun across the table like a stationery shuriken — Suzie was getting to be flamboyant with their dispersal. Sadly, the old fart misjudged the spin and dropped it on the floor. I didn't see him having the stamina to sweep up the card. He left it in the lint.

"Want a shot at another one?" Suzie asked.

"I think I'll give it a miss. So, about the typewriter?"

I passed fingers through my hair, doubtful. "What's the problem?"

"It's driving me to distraction — *clack, clack, clack, whiz-whirl, ka-ching!* at all hours — and then, when I storm in here to discover what the racket is all about, the bastard is docile and calm. Silent, even."

"As all good typewriters should be. What do you think the problem is?" I could be a persistent bugger, and I was guessing senility.

"I haven't a clue — you're the experts."

"Depends if the base issue is metaphysical or medicinal."

"I'm not mad."

"So you're saying it operates itself?"

"Precisely."

"Power surges?"

"This is a manual typewriter. There's no plug. Even so, the bugger starts up anytime it likes, typing away and then hitting return with that stupid bell. *Ding, ding, ding!* I feel like I have a tram in my apartment. It also leaves me messages."

"On the phone?"

"Of course not. It doesn't speak."

"Then it writes to you?"

"Yes, that *is* the inference." Our host was getting irritable. I'd been wondering how long that'd take, and this time there had been remarkably little contribution to the nonsense from the bespectacled blonde on my left. She was gazing over at the typewriter in analysis-mode as the old guy handed me some US Letter-size papers.

On the first was a shopping list, typed in caps — PLEASE BUY: PAPER, RIBBON, CORRECTION FLUID, and something called MAC INE OIL.

"What's 'MAC INE OIL'?"

"Machine oil. I told you — the 'H' sticks."

"So you did. Hurrah," I muttered, putting the list to the back of the pile and examining the next note. "Okay: 'WOULD YOU RUB SOME OF T IS — *this?* — OIL ON MY KEYS?' Pfft. The typewriter has tactile tendencies."

Didn't expect any response to a quip prime-time stupid before it left my lips.

"Can I look, can I look?" Suzie railed from nearby, the goddamn kindergartener.

I put up blinkers as I passed the papers back to our prospective client. Could still make money out of a ruse if I played my cards right. Definitely the man was bonkers, but a rich loon was better than a mad pauper.

"I charge a hundred bucks a day, plus expenses."

"Sounds reasonable. This fee would cover the young lady as well?"

"She's a write-off. Now, is this your typewriter?"

"No. It was my father's."

"Journalist?"

"A writer."

"Classics?"

"Good Lord, hardly. Pulp — the usual kinds of horror, science fiction and detective stories. He made a pretty penny."

"I have to ask. Your old man's passed on?"

This old man cocked his head while pursing lips with a post-lemonish demeanour. "Well, now. What do *you* think?"

"Mm-hmm." Too wizened to punch out and, anyway, I was a century late to play by his Marquess of Queensberry rules. I ignored the tone. "So — he died on the typewriter, or near it?"

"You believe the thing to be possessed?"

"Like you, mate, I haven't the faintest. But please answer the question."

"My father died in a hotel in Reno, on top of a two-dollar hooker."

"Thought you said he avoided the classics?"

"Oh, really now. You have the gumption to call this service?"

"I call it getting a job done."

"Roy. Shhh!" That was Suzie — who else?

I tried not getting annoyed and instead took out a pad to pretend to write. "Father nowhere near typewriter. Two-buck tramp." I rested my hand. "And how often would you say this machine...activates itself? Per day, I mean."

"Once, sometimes twice. Usually at night. The swine likes to keep me guessing."

"Have you tried feeding it?"

Yep, Suzie again, tossing in all thumbs' two cents. The landlord and me combined forces to look over sharply, causing her to blush.

"Ribbon, I mean. *Ribbon.* Jeez, what were you two thinking?"

Time to ignore the girl — surprising, really, how often that occurred. "Why don't you just throw it out?" I suggested.

"What?" David Niven looked horrified.

"Open the window. Pick up the typewriter. Toss it."

"Do you know how irresponsible that is? I live on the fourth floor. What if it landed on someone's skull?"

"Well, all right, if you want to play socially behaved, why not carry the typewriter out of here, down the stairs or in the elevator, and stick it with the trash?"

"I'm eighty-two years old. You try lifting the blighter."

"Sure."

I sauntered over to the bureau. There was an undusted bag of golf clubs leaned against the other side, so I moved this behind me, propped up against the wall. The sun outside was already hightailing. Would be evening in a matter of minutes. I placed the writing pad in my pocket, eased hands beneath the rim of the machine, and hefted — well, tried my darnedest to do so. The monster weighed a ton and hardly budged. Stupid 1940s machinery. I took a step back to survey the situation and when I looked over I spotted a smirk on fossil-man's face.

"Sir, would you mind? We prefer to work in private."

"Certainly, certainly. My poor manners." He lifted his chinless jaw with that smirk and waltzed out in slow motion.

When the door closed, I had my moment. "Prat."

"Smooth," I heard Suzie respond over my shoulder.

Mocking? Oh, man. What kind of rubbishy situation had I stumbled into? A subconscious gnashing of chompers told me it was time to get serious. Again attempting to pick up the typewriter, I accidentally hit the carriage return button. Louder cursing from me swiftly pursued a loud *ka-ching!* — The carriage had hit dead centre of my crown jewels.

Worse still was Suzie's cackling giggle. I felt like pulling out my gun and blowing away either the typewriter or the girl — wasn't sure which would offer the most satisfaction. Probably neither, given the ongoing pain I experienced. "Shut up, will you? Gimme a moment. Crap."

"Double-crap."

That was precisely when Suzie stopped laughing and I ceased breathing, at least for a couple of seconds. Even forgot all about the ache. Something wrong was happening to the typewriter, just as the last wink of direct sunlight disappeared.

Six long, shiny beetle legs — at least a metre apiece — slid out from the machine's casing, and it lifted upright, meaning the metal typewriter was vertical, with the keys positioned precisely where a beer belly'd sit pretty. As for the head that now emerged...fuckit, *was* that a head? Just above the Underwood logo was something looking like a rodent's muzzle, inverted, so there was a hole in the scaly face and two bulbous black peepers that stared straight at me, unblinking.

"Hey," I muttered — some sort of absurd, unintentional greeting — but the bugger was rude and stared without a word. "Ahh, the strong silent type." Very carefully I put my hands behind me, feeling for that dusty bag of golfing irons.

"*Clack, clack,*" the typewriter finally said. Not through the crazy mouth, but via its torso.

"Clack?" Suzie responded.

"*Clack, clack...*clickety-*click-clack!*"

"Talkative bugger, isn't he?" I said. "Suzie, what the fuck is that?"

"Oh, now you need me?"

"Sunshine, let it be said I always need you. I pretend otherwise — image and all." Doubt she believed a word, but I needed speedy facts instead of infantile lip.

The ploy appeared to do the trick.

"Honestly? I'm not quite sure," Suzie said. In the corner of my eye I noticed she edged back, against the wall, but was impressed she held it together. I knew how much the girl detested insects, mice and chickens, and this was one very sorry merger of all three. "Alien infiltration, akin to a hermit crab? Some kind of organic/mechanical hybrid? A rat trapped inside the contraption? Personally, I'm steering toward the first one."

"Remind me again."

"Alien infiltration — strikes me as similar to a report I read about a sentient typewriter in Tangier, though that came down to insecticide the people were inhaling. Could instead be a ghost in the machine?"

This last comment got the blighter typing: "*Click, clack* — ka-ching! *Clackety-clack-click!*"

"Careful with the clichés."

"No ghost? Okay, fair enough. You know — I think it might be attempting to communicate with us in Morse code," Suzie said, just as my fingers behind me sized up a lob wedge.

"Open the window, will you?"

"Oh, sure — it's quite hot, right?" My pretty young assistant yanked up the glass. I noticed there was sweat on her temples. "A little fresh air will do us good while we decide what to do. First of all, is this little man using American Morse code, or Continental German? There is a difference. Hopefully it's the international standard version. Someone, somewhere, has to have a Morse-code guidebook. Easier still to find online. Do you think our client has a PC? I know it's not exactly useful, but if we need to buy a manual we could put in a claim for the purchase with our next tax return, and, well—"

"Six!"

Yep, the choice of the lob wedge was better than the simple brutality of a driving iron. It conjured up a shot with a high arc that took the typewriter over a low bookshelf and the windowsill, clear into the evening air. I heard *clack-clacking* diminish until an explosion of metal hit the ground far below. Hadn't played such a rowdy game of golf since the case of sunstroke.

Suzie jumped to the window and peered down.

"He communicating still?" I asked, merrily returning the club to its bag.

"I can't hear anything."

"Didn't take out any innocent bystanders in the process?"

"I don't know! Too dark down there to see. But it's probably in little pieces."

"You can thank me later."

The girl looked back at me with a perky, annoyed frown.

"You really should learn your correct sporting commentary. That was a golfing shot, yet you resorted to cricket — a 'six' is scored when the ball goes over the boundary rope without touching the ground. No one shouts it out except idle spectators. If it's golf you were mimicking, then you should've shouted out the warning 'fore' — and it's not spelt F-O-U-R but F-O-R-E. Okay?"

"Blah, blah, blah. Write it up in the visitors' book."

"You're completely — *completely* — shameless, Roy. You just destroyed a beautiful antique, and the sentient being that inhabited it. D'you know what we could have learned from this creature?"

"Meh, it prob'ly would've sounded all French to me, the way he kept dropping those H's." I gave her a big sham smile and headed for the door. Time to collect our pay.

The apartment was silent and most of the lights off. David Niven had either done a runner or stepped out for a game of lawn bowls. Either way his wallet'd gone with him.

After taking an old concertina elevator down to the ground floor we walked out and discovered our patron sunbaking on the pavement in the dark, his head sandwiched by a busted up, completely normal-looking 21.5 kg typewriter.

"Oh, Christ," uttered Suzie.

Me? I was transfixed by said spectacle. For the first time in a dog's age no snappy comeback veered my way. Some false teeth lay on a close-by nature strip. I stared in silence, barely able to breathe. A pool of black liquid ran into new cracks in the cement. I'd polished off a bona-fide human being.

"Roy?"

"Screwed," was all I could say.

"Roy." Suzie placed herself between the corpse, the machine, and me. "Roy, you listening to me? Roy!" She slapped me hard, a stinger that struck the left cheek and the corner of my mouth.

"What?" I asked, still vague but slowly focusing on the girl's face before me. There was anger there, also a stubborn purpose I'd never seen Suzie display.

"Snap out of it. Now. We need to move."

"I killed the guy."

"You killed the typewriter. Whether this elderly man and the typewriter were some kind of bizarre kindred spirit, or if he had the bad sense of timing to be passing beneath when you knocked the monster out the window — well, we'll never know and it honestly doesn't matter. Pull yourself together."

"But — I —"

"But *nothing*!" Suzie glared up at me, holding my arms. "We are not going to jail for this, not for doing our job. We're simply going to walk away. To do so I need to tidy up things. What did you touch in the apartment? Roy, what did you touch?"

I tried to look past her. She dodged in the way again. A light rain had started to fall.

"Not there. Look at me. What did you touch?"

"I — the typewriter. The golf club."

"Which one?"

"The typewriter, the one just—"

"*Which* golf club?"

"The lob wedge."

"Right. Nothing else?"

"No." Water dripped down my face but I barely felt it.

Suzie turned on her heel, went to the dead body, and wiped over the fractured pieces of the typewriter with a sleeve. That done, she stood straight to peer up at the building we'd left.

"I'll be back in a few minutes. Don't stray. If any fool stumbles across this mess, we'll meet a block down — thataway." The girl pointed towards the corner of Sholes and Glidden. "Understand?"

I glanced away. "Yeah."

"Roy." Suzie stepped back to me and placed arms around my waist, her face coming close, hair wet. I never noticed before how dazzling she was, even with the glasses spattered by raindrops and one bloody sleeve. "We'll be fine." I heard thunder somewhere distant. Then she winked and headed for the entrance.

"Suze," I called.

She stopped to look at me, a resourceful smile on her lips. "What?"

"Don't forget the business card the old coot dropped."

"*Mmm*. That's more like the Roy I cherish."

ghouls' glossary

Aussie vernacular, places, products & people, along with music, some written matter, horror shop-talk, and the odd film you might want to brush up on—or not.

Action Comics: American comic-book series that introduced Superman

Antioch: an ancient Greek city on the eastern side of the Orontes River. Its ruins lie near the modern city of Antakya, Turkey

Australian Ballet: largest ballet company in Australia, established in 1962

BB-gun: a type of air gun designed to fire spherical projectiles similar to shot pellet

Brekky: breakfast

Chandler, Raymond: American novelist & screenwriter most famous for hard-boiled detective character Philip Marlowe

Chaney, Jr., Lon: played the Wolf Man, the Mummy & Frankenstein's Monster in horror from Universal Studios in the 1930s/40s

Colt 1911 .45: semi-automatic pistol produced by Colt from 1911

Compact discs (CDs): digital optical disc data storage format launch in early 1980s

Converse All Stars: canvas & rubber shoes first produced in 1917

Cushing, Peter: English actor famous in Hammer Films & as Grand Moff Tarkin in *Star Wars* Episode IV

Dunny: toilet

Fed Ex: a.k.a. Federal Express, a speedy international courier service

Flinders Street Station: central railway station in Melbourne, opened 1854

Foghorn Leghorn: American cartoon rooster appearing in Warner Bros. shorts

'**Fountain':** Marcel Duchamp's 1917 display of a porcelain urinal

Ghost gum: evergreen tree native to Australia, with white to cream and pink-tinged bark

Hammer Films: British film company founded in 1934, famous for horror in the 1950s-70s

Hammett, Dashiell: American author of hard-boiled detective novels and short stories, famous for Sam Spade & the Continental Op

Hudson, Rock: Hollywood actor, born Roy Harold Scherer, Jr. Famous for *Pillow Talk, Giant* & *McMillan & Wife*

Jackson, Michael: American singer/songwriter & former member of Jackson 5

***Kolchak: The Night Stalker*:** early '70s movies, and then a single-season TV series 1974-75

Lawson, Henry: famous Australian writer/poet of the colonial period

Lee, Christopher: English actor famous in Hammer Films as Dracula & later in the *Lord of the Rings* trilogy.

'**Loaded Dog, The':** farcical Henry Lawson short story published in Australia in 1901

Loo: Toilet

McGavin, Darren: American actor best known for *Kolchak* and the 1950s version of Mickey Spillane's Mike Hammer

Mifune, Toshiro: Japanese actor, famous for samurai roles in *Seven Samurai* & *Yojimbo*

Moneypenny, Miss: M's secretary in the James Bond novels & movies

Price, Vincent: American actor, known for distinctive voice & performances in horror

Renfield: lunatic asylum inmate under the influence of the Count in Bram Stoker's *Dracula*

Runners: in Australian English used for 'sneakers'

Saint James, Susan: American actor/activist, born Susan Jane Miller & famous for *McMillan & Wife*

Small Change: 1976 album released through Asylum Records by Tom Waits

Smith & Wesson: U.S. firearms manufacturer founded in 1852

Spillane, Mickey: American author of crime novels, famous for Mike Hammer

Steely Dan: American jazz rock band founded in 1972

Stoker, Bram: Irish novelist best known for 1897 gothic novel *Dracula*

Supermundane: above and beyond the nature or character of the worldly or terrestrial

Ta: thanks

Underwood: a manufacturer of typewriters headquartered in New York City

Unreal: unbelievable, but equally often fantastic

Uzi: Israeli open-bolt, blowback-operated submachine gun

Vegemite: popular Australian salty black spread—put on toast for brekky

VHS: Video Home System analogue recording videotape created by Victor, Japan

Victoria Street: famous for a concentration of Vietnamese restaurants & shops in Richmond, Melbourne

Video Girl Ai: manga series created in 1989 by Masakazu Katsura and published by Shueisha's Weekly Shōnen Jump

Waits, Tom: American singer-songwriter, composer & actor

Western Star: Australian brand of butter, est. 120 years ago

You Only Live Twice: 1967 James Bond movie, with 007 in Japan

ACKNOWLEDGEMENTS

If you feel the need to go blame something for the casebook you've just read, I wouldn't target either Roy or Suzie. Nor should you bludgeon me—blame instead the act of growing up on cross-media cultural oddities in 1970s Melbourne (and briefly up on the Gold Coast) sourced from the USA, the UK, Japan, and back home.

So, where to start?

I suppose I've got to raise a hat to the 'odd couple' trope established early on in cinema by matching Bob with Bing, Bogie and Lorre, Dean riding Jerry, Mifune getting to trade swords with Shimura, or Robbie the Robot making drinks for Earl Holliman (that last one was in the great *Forbidden Planet*).

British TV continued the vibe via *Steptoe and Son* and various hangers-on provided to the good Doctors Who, Jon Pertwee and Tom Baker.

One of the greatest offbeat couplings matched neat, uptight Felix Unger with slovenly Oscar Madison in Neil Simon's 1965 play *The Odd Couple*—I grew up on the film (1968) and spin-off series.

But my favourite odd couple as a kid were married: Susan Saint James and Rock Hudson starred in *McMillan & Wife* from 1971-77. They didn't bicker anywhere near as much as Roy and Suzie in this book, but I was enamoured with their contrasting personalities, a blasé sense of humour, and the fact they were often sidetracked in attempts to solve crime.

Plus there was Mildred, their boozing maid, and the bumbling Sergeant Enright.

Add to this a steady childhood diet of *The Outer Limits* and Rod Serling personally presenting *The Twilight Zone* while smoking cigarettes—along with Australia's answer to both series in *The Evil Touch*, hosted by Anthony Quayle. Plus one-off TV horror gems like *Trilogy of Terror* and midnight movie re-runs of classic Hammer Films and American International flicks—which starred luminaries Vincent Price, Christopher Lee, Ingrid Pitt and Peter Cushing.

American producers Sid and Marty Krofft's *H.R. Pufnstuf* and *Land of the* Lost veered close to a kind of bizarre, whacked-out soft-horror for children, while in 1960s British series *The Avengers* and its '70s replacement *The New Avengers* actors like Patrick Macnee, Diana Rigg, Gareth Hunt and Joanna Lumley were always fighting off kitsch-looking monsters.

Top of this superb heap was *Kolchak: The Night Stalker*, which started out as two movies and ran as a single-season series (1974-75) yet never left the reruns on Australian tellies. Man, I still dig this show.

Meanwhile, during daytime hours, I was flicking through comic books such as DC's *Weird War*, the long-running *Creepy* series through Warren, Eerie's *Tales of Voodoo*, and *Ripley's Believe It or Not* via Gold Key; hooked to oddball art by Steve Ditko, Jack Kirby, Barry (Windsor) Smith, Kazuo Umezu and Jim Steranko.

People like Sam Raimi, Jess Whedon, Tim Burton and Darren McGavin have reinforced the fact that you can indeed have fun with horror—but if you look back a hundred years, what is Marcel Duchamp's 'Fountain' if not a scathing pisstake of the horror that is serious art?

For me hardboiled/noir drifts so well into the soft-horror construct, probably because the novels I've read most times over are by Raymond Chandler (*The Big Sleep*, *The Long Goodbye*) and Dashiell Hammett (*The Maltese Falcon*, *The Thin Man*, *Red Harvest*). If you haven't read any of these books, and you want to take something of value out of this experience, go grab them. Now.

Anyway, Roy and Suzie first appeared as an "item" in the *Pulp Ink 2* anthology published in 2012 (the zombie yarn that begins this book) and I loved working with the pair so much that

I did over a dozen more stories. From late 2013, they started to appear as recurring characters—surprisingly popular—in the IF? Commix publication *Tales to Admonish*, where Matt Kyme and Adam Rose drew them.

While I wrote the R&S tales I did retain a conscious chronology, a timeline in which the actions take place: early Roy experiences wth Arthur—Suzie's dad—along with a middle period when Suzie first replaces Art. The later period, in which the two central characters finally, against all odds, warm to one another, was always going to be the closing bracket—just like in traditional odd-couple romps.

I also threw a bit of a Raymond Chandler and cannibalized stories featuring other characters (Floyd and Laurel from *Tobacco-Stained Mountain Goat*, for instance) to add some depth to the experience, and constructed linking moments in order to give the casebook better flow. It all ends with my favourite Roy & Suzie story, which originally was published in a Crime Factory anthology in Australia—and a heady salute must be given here to editor Liam José, who recommended the twist in the relationship at the finale.

I can't imagine it any other way now.

Finally, there are particular people I need to thank for helping to nurture the Roy & Suzie experience in order to reach the collected book form currently in your hands: First up, Dominic @ John Hunt, who agreed to run with the novel—and has helped so much with my previous Perfect Edge titles. Further thanks to the editors of the anthologies *Pulp Ink 2* (Nigel Bird and Chris Rhatigan), *Weird Noir* (Kate Laity), *Horror Factory* (Liam José), and *Somewhere in the Shadows*, along with the publishers of these books. Big cheers go out to Matt Kyme and Adam Rose for giving these characters actual faces on-page in *Tales to Admonish*. Arigato to Renee Pickup, who ran with two stories for the Hallowe'en specials on Revolt Daily, while Christopher Mattick demanded a Roy & Suzie Facebook presence and Steven Alloway never stopped loving the two characters—letting other people know that via Fanboy Comics. Others deserving of praise include Adam Jack, Galo Gutierrez, Ben Kooyman, Tim Feely, Gary Mackries, Shawn Vogt, John Kowalski, Nevada McPherson, Warren Dusting, Seb Bayne, Brian Huber, Greg Burgas @ CBR, David Foster, John Hamilton, Dan Leicht, Anthony Castle, Fiona McDroll, Elizabeth A. White, Heath Lowrance, Paul Bowler @ Sci-Fi Jubilee, Comic Bastards, Geeks of Doom, All-Comic, Ceej @ Big Comic Page, Pipedream, and Joe Grunewald @ NerdSpan.

Any list must also include the readers of the comics as much as the short stories, who either let me know their feelings or reviewed for the media.

Cheers going out to friends and family who (a) helped defined what and who I am, and thereby the style you find here—so blame them too!—as well as supporting the projects I waste time with now.

Especially Yoko and Cocoa.

Finally? I'd already decided on the title of this novel—*Small Change*—a few months back, an homage to the great Tom Waits 1976 LP as much as it was a reference to the short nature of each of Roy's narrated tales making up the casebook.

When I googled the title, I straight away ran up against the wunderbar artwork of Alec Goss—whose *Small Change* painting now graces the cover.

Andrez Bergen,
Tokyo 2015

DEPTH CHARGING ICE PLANET GOTH
(2014)

"From goth coming-of-age to violently gothic, Andrez Bergen wanted his own style mixed with a bit of Edgar Allan Poe — and got the recipe spot on." **THE BOOKBAG**

"A trippy little book about teenage rage and righteousness. Think cult classic film *Heathers* with a healthy heap of *Alice in Wonderland*, and you've got the idea." **THE NEXT BEST BOOK CLUB**

"I was totally blown away... his best tale to date." **WEIRD AND WONDERFUL READS**

"Just finished *Depth Charging Ice Planet Goth* — and it's a great, wild, heartfelt, heartbreaking, wonderful novel. Endlessly creative." **JOSH STALLINGS (author, *Beautiful, Naked & Dead*)**

"A coming-of-age novel seen through the eyes of a tormented child trying to become an adult... The perfect storm for Andrez Bergen that has this Christopher Nolan puzzle-like quality to it." **DEAD END FOLLIES**

"Andrez Bergen introduces us to his most remarkable character to date in a dark, gothic tale — truly fabulous storytelling, and to my mind the author's best." **IN GLORIOUS TECHNICOLOR**

"A fascinating and quirky character." **THE CULT DEN**

"There's a lot at work in this story: loss, love, and more than a smidgeon of lunacy, making it one of the most refreshing reads of 2014." **DORK SHELF**

"An enthralling tale of survival, endurance, and coming-of-age."
OZNOIR

"I don't think I've ever read a book quite like this one. It's odd and unique, at times funny, at times poignant, but always compelling." **FANBOY COMICS**

"I love the fusion feel of this book. I love how it proudly cross pollinates comic style blunt with coming of age literature — so much is great about *DCIPG*. I think I might fancy Anim too!" **JONNY GIBBINGS (author, *Malice in Blunderland*)**

She's a disturbed, quiet girl, but Mina wants to do some good
out there. It's just that the world gets in the way. This is
Australia in the 1980s, a haven for goths and loners, where a
coming-of-age story can only veer into a murder mystery.

ISBN-13: 978-1782796497

WHO IS KILLING THE GREAT CAPES OF HEROPA? (2013)

"Pulp fiction brought bang up to date and then slammed hard into the roots of its own mythology." **AVAILABLE IN ANY COLOUR**

"Incredibly engaging, clever and a fantastic piece of escapism — simply super." **SF BOOK REVIEWS**

"A mixed-media love letter to the golden age of comics and the classic detective story." **JOE CLIFFORD (author, *Junkie Love*)**

"Super-powered superhero literature and comic-book goodness." **SOLARCIDE**

"That this story about comics should be so similar to a murder mystery of the Sam Spade kind is just the cherry on the cake." **THE MOMUS REPORT**

"The best non-comic-book superhero story I've ever read." **COMIC BASTARDS**

"Like a crazy, post-modern road trip with Jack Kirby riding shotgun, and everyone from Stan Lee to Raymond Chandler nattering away in the back seat." **THE THRILLING DETECTIVE**

"Terrific, postmodern superhero noir." **JASON FRANKS (author, *McBlack*)**

"Vintage pulp-dieselpunk-superhero action at its finest!" **DAILY STEAMPUNK**

"Any writer who can pull twists and a mystery like that deserves recognition and a ton of praise." **ACERBIC WRITING**

"Deconstructs what it means to be a hero." **DORK SHELF**

"A highly stylized, retro-futuristic world." **SF SIGNAL**

"Excellent." **THE FOUNDING FIELDS**

"I very much doubt I'll read a better supers novel." **THE NAMELESS HORROR**

"Tough stuff with a golden heart." **I MEANT TO READ THIS**

"These are superheroes at their best and worst, just like Lee and Kirby intended them to be." **JOHN KOWALSKI @ WORD OF THE NERD**

"One wild trip." **GEEK MAGAZINE**

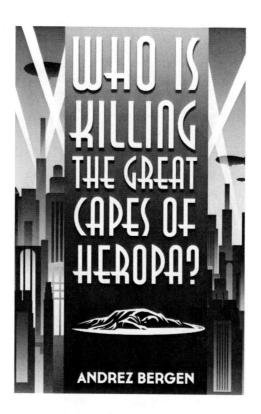

Heropa: A vast, homogenized city patrolled by heroes and
populated by adoring masses. A pulp-fiction fortress of solitude
for crime-fighting team the Equalizers, led by new recruit
Southern Cross — a lifetime away from the rain-drenched,
dystopic metropolis of Melbourne.
Who, then, is killing the great Capes of Heropa?
In this paired homage to detective noir from the 1940s and the
'60s Marvel age of trailblazing comic books, Andrez Bergen
gloriously redefines the mild-mannered superhero novel.

ISBN-13: 978-1782792352

ONE HUNDRED YEARS OF VICISSITUDE
(2012)

"Charles Dickens collides with Haruki Murakami in a pulsating tale of history, redemption and revenge."
FANTASY BOOK REVIEW

"A wildly enchanting journey down the rabbit hole."
ELIZABETH A. WHITE

"A cracking great story."
BRITISH FANTASY SOCIETY

"Dreamlike and bewitchingly evocative."
THE FLAWED MIND

"A unique, memorable story — indescribable, exhilarating."
FORCES OF GEEK

"Quirky, poignant, and utterly brilliant."
DRYING INK

"Reaffirms a postmodern dexterity of Cirque du Soleil proportions."
FARRAGO MAGAZINE

"Breathtakingly detailed. I defy you to read this book."
STEAMPUNK MAGAZINE

"Exquisite, incredibly touching and devastating in its beauty."
I MEANT TO READ THAT

"A terrific book!"
BARE*BONES

"Crime, geisha, time travel; masterfully balances these things and turns its nose up at pretentious literature."
INSOMNIA PRESS

"A wonderful tale... This is what good literary fiction reads like."
ALWAYSUNMENDED

"A witty voyage of ideas, history, pop culture, style, characters and scenes that are unforgettable."
RAYMOND EMBRACK

"I love this. The narrator is fascinating — as are his two unlikely companions."
LITREACTOR

"Bergen relishes wacky tangents and dives head-first into philosophical dialogues that prove to be some of the most satisfying parts of his books."
DEATH BY KILLING

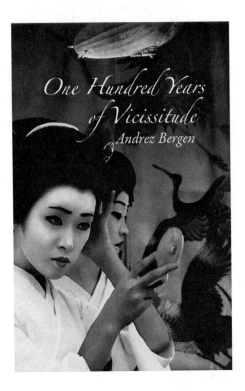

"First up, a disclaimer. I suspect I am a dead man. I have meagre proof, no framed-up certification, nothing to toss in a court of law as evidence of a rapid departure from the mortal coil. I recall a gun was involved, pressed up against my skull, and a loud explosion followed."

Thus begins our narrator in a purgatorial tour through twentieth-century Japanese history, with a ghostly geisha who has seen it all as a guide and a corrupt millionaire as her reluctant companion.

Thrown into the milieu are saké, B-29s, Lewis Carroll, Sir Thomas Malory, Melbourne, *The Wizard of Oz*, and a dirigible — along with the allusion that Red Riding Hood might just be involved.

ISBN-13: 978-1780995977

about the author

Andrez Bergen is an expat Australian writer, journalist, artist and DJ from Melbourne, entrenched in Tokyo these past 14 years.

He published his debut novel *Tobacco-Stained Mountain Goat* in 2011, followed by *One Hundred Years of Vicissitude* (2012), *Who is Killing the Great Capes of Heropa?* (2013), and *Depth Charging Ice Planet Goth* (2014).

He has also written and produced artwork for two graphic novels (an adaptation of *Tobacco-Stained Mountain Goat*, and *Bullet Gal*) and published other comics and short stories through Perfect Edge Books, Under Belly Comics, Crime Factory, Snubnose Press, Shotgun Honey, 8th Wonder Press, IF? Commix, Big Pulp, Dirty Rotten Comics, and Another Sky Press.

He further co-edited an anthology of post-apocalyptic noir.

On the side, Bergen worked on adapting scripts for feature films by Mamoru Oshii (*Ghost in the Shell*), Kazuchika Kise and Naoyoshi Shiotani at Production I.G.

He additionally hammers together tunes as Little Nobody, he

covets sashimi and saké, and lives in Japan with his wife and nine-year-old daughter Cocoa.

andrezbergen.wordpress.com
Illustration by Adam Rose

At Roundfire we publish great stories. We lean towards the spiritual and thought-provoking. But whether it's literary or popular, a gentle tale or a pulsating thriller, the connecting theme in all Roundfire fiction titles is that once you pick them up you won't want to put them down.